# Better Days

## Quinn Miller

Better Days
Copyright © 2021 by Quinn Miller
All rights reserved.

Cover Design by Shannon Passmore of Shanoff Designs
Edited by Sandra Dee of One Love Editing
& Christina Hart of Savage Hart Book Services
Proofread by Amanda Cuff of Savage Hart Book Services
& Christina Hart of Savage Hart Book Services
First Edition Formatted by J.R. Rogue of Savage Hart Book Services
Second Edition Formatted by Victoria Ellis of Cruel Ink Publishing

ISBN: 9798595227629

*To my husband and daughters.*
*You are forever my reasons why.*
*Thank you for your support and encouragement.*

# PROLOGUE

## Jules

*G*od. So much can change in under an hour.

Matt gazes up at me as he slides his black athletic shorts back on, still shirtless, which is so distracting. "It suits you."

*He is sitting on my bed.* The little girl in me wants to scream and dance around my room. I've been crushing on him since he became best friends with my older brother. I always hoped he'd see me as more than just his best friend's little sister, but I never actually thought it would happen. And now, he's sitting on my sea-green ombré sheets—the duvet scrunched at the end of my bed, my throw pillows on the floor.

My bedroom has changed a little since I was twelve, when my main Christmas present was a room makeover. Five years later, as I glance around, it suddenly seems so different.

I look back at Matt and smile. "Don't shrug and give me a non-answer. Why did you call me *butterfly*, Matthew Gregory?"

"That's what you are. My butterfly."

"Of all the things you could call me, why that?"

Before he can reply, we hear honking outside. We both know it's my brother, Mitch, signaling for Matt to come out. Our time is up.

Mitch and Matt became best friends the moment they met. Matt has been a part of my life ever since. If my brother knew—not only that we like each other, but also what we just did—honestly, I have no clue what he'd do. I worry his friendship with Matt would be over.

Matt shoots up as he pulls his shirt on. "Maybe Mitch didn't think it was odd I stayed back here to do homework while he went to Hannah's, but he'll definitely find it odd if he finds me half-dressed in here with his sister."

He's right. My brother's been too wrapped up with his girlfriend, Hannah, to pay us much attention. He didn't question it when Matt stayed here to do homework and asked my brother to swing back and pick him up for practice. But if he walked in on us right now, there'd be no disguising what just happened.

With long strides, Matt heads to leave. After stopping at the door, he walks back over, puts his finger under my chin, and tilts my head up toward him. I look into those incredible blue eyes that make me forget all thoughts.

"No regrets, okay? Yes, we have things to figure out—the main one being your brother. But I am not sorry this happened. Far from it. I don't want you to be, either. I don't know how all of this will work, but it *will* work. I hate that I have to leave now, but I better go."

I feel like there's more he wants to say. As I study him, seeing the sincerity on his face, it stops me from muttering a smartass remark or pushing him for more.

"Okay, we'll talk later," I whisper. I want to say so much more, but now isn't the time. We'll have time later.

I close my bedroom door as he leaves, resting my head

against it afterward. I can't stop the obnoxious grin from overtaking my face. Today is *the* most memorable day of my life.

I had sex for the first time. With my brother's best friend. My first love. God, I haven't told him that—*yet*. But I feel it. I may only be seventeen, but I *know* I love him. Maybe, just maybe, he loves me too.

Matt runs downstairs to get in the car with my brother. I promise myself the next time we have a moment, I'll tell him. Right now, they have to rush off to football practice. It's their senior year, and their team has a decent shot at a championship. I'm one year younger, so they'll both be leaving me next year for college.

It was surely stupid of me to start something with Matt, considering. But right now, I don't care. Next year, when I'm all alone, I may feel differently.

As Matt and my brother head off to practice, I put my bed— and myself—back together. My mom will be home from work soon. *I can do this.* I can act as if nothing has changed. I can have him in my house practically all the time and not want to repeat what just happened. I look around the room once more, remembering what Matt and I just did, and smile. *Shit. I am so screwed.*

After I finish my homework, I go down to see my mom, knowing she's already home by now. I find her in the kitchen, where I hop up on the counter. "Anything I can help with for dinner?"

"Why did Mitch have to swing back here to get Matt?" she asks me with a smirk, ignoring my question.

"What?"

She gives me a knowing glance.

I think she has her suspicions about us, but she has no idea how far things have actually gone. She loves Matt, but I don't know what she'd think about me dating Mitch's best friend. Unfortunately, they are the same person. Right now, it sucks that he can't just be *mine*.

Matt told me months ago he couldn't stop thinking about me, that he has feelings for me. My mom is big on family loyalty. Matt and Mitch have been joined at the hip since the fourth grade. If we were to date, it would change things. Not only for my brother and Matt, but likely for everyone. Once the boys became close, our families started hanging out together and now, even our parents are dear friends.

So, yeah, the *change* aspect...that's the part my mom might have a problem with. But we will figure it out. We have to.

I like him too much to give him up. We'll work it all out.

I hate lying, so I stare at my phone like I'm searching for something in order to avoid looking at my mom. "Oh. I think Matt had to finish up some homework, so Mitch swung back home after hanging with *Hannah*."

My mom laughs at me and says, "Jules. Your eyes are too pretty to spend so much time in the back of your head, sweetheart."

"What?" I put my phone screen-side down and shrug.

"Your eye roll."

"Ugh. You are the second person to comment on my eye rolling today. I do not roll my eyes a lot. It's Hannah's fault. She brings it out of me with her *nasty* attitude. What my brother sees in her, I have no idea."

Well, that isn't completely true. I know what he sees in her. She's beautiful. But to me, her fakeness and gossipy nature detract from her beauty.

"Second person, huh? Who, pray tell, was the other one, daughter of mine?" my mom says with a *gotcha* look.

*Yeah, she definitely knows something.*

Trying to change my mom's focus from me, I look to check the time. "Is Mitch coming home or going back to Hannah's after dropping Matt off at his house? Their practice ended a while ago." I hop down from the counter and pick up the washed lettuce to make the salad for dinner.

"He texted me and asked if Matt could have dinner here, so they should both be here any minute," my mom says, with another little smirk.

Wanting to avoid any further questions, I focus on my phone for real this time, confused when I see I have seventeen text messages. There's one from Matt, but it's the others that draw my attention first. Texts asking if I'm okay and that they're so sorry to hear about my brother.

"What the fuck?"

"Jules, language," scolds my mom.

But I'm too preoccupied to care about my language in front of her. I have text after text from friends, some from numbers I don't even know, saying they heard about the accident. *What accident?*

That question is answered by the second to last text. It has a video attachment and one awful question: *"Is this your brother's car?"*

My finger hovers over the tiny box. Something so simple seems to take so much strength. I tap it to make the video go full screen. Before I play it, our landline rings.

Seven seconds. That's how long I take to put my cell down and reach for the home phone. I didn't know it yet, but those seven seconds would be the last bit of everything I'd known. *Seven seconds.* Then, everything would change.

I beat my mom to the phone. If the Redmond rumor mill is correct and quick on spreading news, I have to protect her, even if it's just for a few more moments.

"Hello?"

"Hello, Kathleen? It's Trish, Hannah's mom."

"Actually, this is Jules. Is there something I can help you with?"

Her voice is struggling. It sounds like she's trying not to break on the phone with me as she stops and starts twice before saying, "Oh, sweetie. I am so sorry. Can I speak with your mom?"

I hand the phone to my mother as she eyes me curiously.

I can only hear my mom's side of the conversation, but I can tell by how her face falls that the text messages must be true. My brother has been in an accident.

My mom crumbles, landing in the oddest position on the floor. I keep thinking she must be so uncomfortable with her legs like that. The noises coming from her will forever be imprinted in my memories.

I take the phone from my mom's limp hand to see if Trish has hung up. My voice cracks. "He-hello?" I'm not sure how I'm holding it together as well as I am. But I shake my head and try to deal with this since my mom seems incapable.

"I'm still here, honey. I'm so sorry to have to do this. I don't know if your mom heard everything I said. I hate to ask this of you, but can you help your mom out the door? You guys need to get to the hospital." I can hear her stuttered breaths. "Hannah was following Mitch and saw everything. I called you as soon as I got off the call with her."

I look down at my mom and stroke the top of her head. Taking a deep breath, I try to calm my pulse. "Thank you for calling." I don't wait to hear if Hannah's mom has anything additional to say. I hang up and instantly call my dad.

He's still at his office, working late. He picks up on the first ring.

"Daddy..."

WALKING into the hospital makes things real. A few minutes after I spoke with my dad, the police called. Even then, things seemed a bit faraway. Our neighbor, Becky, came over after my dad called her. Between the two of us, we had to guide my mom through the motions. I think my mom felt things were faraway too.

I haven't cried yet. Is that wrong? Maybe not wrong, but odd. It doesn't seem normal, that's for sure.

The energy and sheer anxiety level in the emergency room make me stoic. Things need to be handled, and as we help my mom sit down, I realize she lacks the strength to do so on her own. I walk up to the admin window with my mom's purse, where I inquire about my brother's condition and offer his insurance card. I hate the way the nurse is watching me. Like I'm fragile. I try to stand straighter and roll my shoulders back.

After a few minutes, a nurse leads us to a private room. Based on binge-watching medical dramas, private rooms are never a good sign. I keep wringing my wrist as I walk into the room.

"Mrs. Morgan, I'm sorry for keeping you waiting. My name is Dr. Emory. I'm overseeing your son's care." She reaches her hand out for my mom, but she just sits there. The awkwardness stretches, so I reach over and shake the woman's outstretched hand.

As I release her hand and go to sit, the door flies open and my dad rushes in. Whatever strength my mom was exhibiting—which wasn't much—leaves once my father's arms wrap around her. We all listen as the doctor calmly lists all of Mitch's injuries. Things sound so grim.

"The next twenty-four hours are critical. But I want you to prepare yourselves. Mitch's injuries are life-threatening."

As she gets up to leave, panic hits me. *Matt.* Oh my God, how did I not think of him before? No one has mentioned him. I stand to stop the doctor.

"Wait. Matt. Was Matt in the car? How is he? He was the passenger in the car, maybe." I spit it all out like it's one question and try sucking in air.

Dr. Emory looks to my parents, then to me. She gives a small smile, but it's only with her lips, no light in her eyes. "I'm sorry. Because of privacy policies, I can't disclose information on another patient."

"Patient. So, he is here. He was in the car." I flop back down in my chair and pull my cell out to text Eric—Matt's younger brother. He and I are in the same grade.

Before I finish the text, we hear animalistic noises coming from the next room. Whoever is on the other side, you can just tell they're being told horrible news. The wails remind me of the sounds my mom made on the call with Trish. As I listen to the cries, I turn my head back toward the doctor and watch her give us a nod and leave the room.

"I need some air," I squeak out. I'll finish my text out there.

As I rush from the room with my head down, the door to the room next to us opens and I run into Bill Gregory, Matt's dad. His eyes are swollen and red-rimmed. He appears emotionally beaten. I can still hear the howling from inside that room. As the door closes, I glimpse Eric comforting his mom while she sobs. I glance from the door to Mr. Gregory and back to the door, before reality settles in, feeling like a thousand-pound weight on my chest.

"Umm, Jules, I...I—" He wipes his hand down his face and looks up to the ceiling. "How's Mitch?"

"We don't know. Something about twenty-four hours. Mr. Gregory..." I shift from one foot to the other, swaying a bit. "Matt?" is all I can get out. I can't ask what I need to.

"Oh, Jules." He gapes at me, his chin trembling, and closes his eyes with tears cascading down his stubble. He shakes his head once.

He doesn't need to finish. My heart already knows.

I don't say anything to him. I don't go to him and try to comfort him. I run. I run as fast as I can until I'm outside with the crisp fall air expanding my lungs. With my hands on my knees, I bend over and vomit. All the stress from the night. All of my emotions from the entire day.

Everything I've stuffed down so I could deal with things and be strong for my mom comes up until I have nothing left but tears. My phone pings with a text message.

It's my dad, looking for me. As I tap the speech bubble to pull up my messages, I see all the texts from earlier, before *everything* changed. And below those is the last text from Matt. My thumb hovers over it, ready to expand the message, but I can't do it. Not yet.

I close my eyes and wish to go back to being in the kitchen with my mom when we were laughing.

God. So much can change in under an hour. In the worst way imaginable.

# 1

## JULES
## PRESENT

*I*t's been a long week. Sadly, I felt that way halfway through Tuesday. Finally, Friday evening has arrived, but the last thing I want to do is put effort into looking cute and going out. My third year as a kindergarten teacher is off to a favorable start, though. I never thought I'd love being called *Ms. Morgan* as much as I do. Although my kids usually just call me *teacher*.

I step over my tote filled with the kids' work I need to go over this weekend and move to the big, beautiful windows in my bedroom. As I peer out at the street, I'm thankful the original windows were left in here when this old home was converted into apartments. I love watching the leaves on the enormous trees right outside change colors.

I thought my love affair with fall would diminish after the accident. Thankfully, it didn't. My chest gets a little tighter around this time of year, though. I think that's normal.

My brother passed away the morning after the accident. I woke to a world that no longer included my brother. Or the boy I loved.

Afterward, my parents were zombies. It was easy to talk them into letting me get my GED and start college a year early. I kept pushing myself forward and reached my dream of teaching.

I attended a school close to home, so I'd be there to help them. When it was time to find a job, the principal at the school I did my student teaching at knew I was seeking not only a job but also a new adventure. She told me a friend of hers was hiring in Portland. She put us in touch, and with her recommendation, I got an interview. Followed by an offer. So, I accepted the teaching position and moved here to Portland.

My mom wasn't happy with my move. The plan had always been to go back home and teach in Redmond. But that was the plan of a love-struck girl. That stopped being me long ago.

Since losing Mitch, she's held on tighter to me. I needed distance to make my own life work. I don't go back home as often as my parents would like. Holidays, mostly. Redmond is just a three-hour drive from Portland, but I've enjoyed the freedom of being away from everything there.

Eric and I still text; he sometimes makes the occasional phone call. I've seen him a handful of times during trips back to Redmond. It's weird for me, though. He isn't like Matt at all, but being around him reminds me of his brother, and that always hurts.

I play with my bracelet on my right wrist. Bella—one of my students—made it for me. It's valuable in sentiment, purely. A string with a couple of beads on it is all. Simple. Every morning, though, when I stand outside our room to greet the kids, she gives me the best smile when she spots it on my wrist.

Gretchen—my best friend and roommate—calls it my *worry bracelet*. She claims she knows I'm deep in thought whenever she catches me playing with the beads.

We found this magnificent apartment in the heart of everything, close to the school we work at in the Mississippi area of

Portland. While I teach kindy, Gretchen teaches first grade. We quickly bonded my first year at the elementary school, and I'm so grateful for her friendship. However, she's also the reason I'm currently playing with my bracelet.

A friend of hers recently opened a bar within walking distance from our place. She's been begging me for weeks to go check it out, so I promised her I'd go tonight. *Why did I promise her?*

I don't mind being social. My private life could use some action. Honestly, it might call for a defibrillator at this point. Gretchen made me set up a profile on a dating app she heard great things about. It isn't my thing, but she sold me on it when she said the app could give me control. I was horrible at putting down what I like and want. I don't want a relationship. The occasional hookup is just fine with me.

But tonight isn't about me or my lackluster dating life; Gretchen wants to support her friend. I sense there's more to it, though. For someone who usually exudes confidence, she seems to need support going to this bar. I was shocked she wouldn't go on her own or with a date. Maybe she likes the guy who owns the bar. She dates often but never seems to get serious with anyone.

As I walk out of my room to go find Gretchen, I holler, "So, tell me again how you know this guy?" I've asked so many times, I'm just playing dumb now.

She gives the same response every time, but I keep hoping I'll trip her up and she'll say something like, *"I'm secretly in love with him and want to have all his babies."* It hasn't happened yet.

Gretchen sighs. "Do you ever listen? We went to school together."

"Is he an ex?" I tease, as I stand in front of her.

She takes a deep breath and looks down. "No."

"That wasn't convincing."

She glances up and gives a small smile. "I thought for a hot second maybe there was something there, but it was years ago. He's never thought of me like that. He's put me solidly in the friend zone." Her voice seems tiny and sad.

As I look at her, I think any man would be an idiot not to think of her *like that*. "Hey, no sadness. His loss if he can't see how incredible you are. But...question. Why are we going, exactly? If he's some guy that makes you feel sad, why don't we watch a movie in tonight instead?"

Gretch looks like she's a million miles away. "For now, can we just leave it as he's a friend? I want to be there for him. He doesn't exactly make me sad. If I'm being perfectly honest, sometimes seeing him is hard. So, I'd like your company to make it easier. Please?" She looks at me hopefully.

I'm always there for her, as she is for me. I don't need any magic words from her to make me go. I will go, for her. "I'll go with you, but I'm telling you now, I'm not putting out," I joke, trying to lighten the mood.

She smiles at me and gives me a hug. As she pulls away, she looks out the window. "Do you want to get a ride or walk? Just trying to figure out if I need a jacket."

I follow her line of sight and see the windows covered in raindrops. "Let's order a ride. Who knows when the rain will start again. I'll get it on my app."

An hour later, we're looking our best. Now that I'm dressed, I'm excited for the evening. I pride myself on not looking like the teachers I grew up with—no sweater sets or long, boring dresses. I must admit, even though I wasn't in the mood to go out, a night in such a fun city has me feeling better and less stressed. My favorite tight black skirt and off-the-

BETTER DAYS | 19

shoulder gray sweater paired with my new black booties have me feeling confident.

As we walk into Portland Social, I instantly like the vibe of the place. "What's your friend's name again?"

"Chase." She nods her head to the guy behind the impressive wood bar with what looks like an inlay of ice facing toward the customer side.

I can see why Gretch wanted backup; Chase is an incredibly good-looking guy. His dark hair has a wave to it. From what I can see, his upper chest and forearms are covered in tattoos. Ink rarely does anything for me, but on him, it's sexy. Though, the most alluring part of him is his cocky grin.

He does a quick scan over the room, and it's obvious when he notices Gretchen. I don't know what flits over his face; but if I had to guess, I'd say her assumption that he isn't interested in her is far from the truth. There's something more in his eyes. A mixture of desire and...what maybe looks like regret.

"Well, don't look now, but the hot bartender is staring at you like he wants to strip you of your clothing and mix a cocktail on you and lick it off."

Gretchen breaks their stare to look at me. She laughs. "What does that even mean? And no, he isn't. Chase is a great guy, okay? Be nice."

We walk over to the bar and find one unoccupied stool. I tell Gretchen to take it; I'll stand until something else opens up. With my elbows on the bar, we wait for Chase to grace us with his presence. If I wasn't positive something was between Gretchen and him, I'd put myself out there.

I haven't truly been with anyone since Matt. Sex is one thing. Giving my time and heart is a completely different beast. Pathetic? Maybe. But it's safe this way. If I don't let a guy into my heart, he can't shatter it. But I still have a pulse, and the desire to *physically* be with someone can be overwhelming.

Vibrators are great, and mine does its job. But, the touch of a man is something it can't give me.

Chase makes his way toward us, and his husky voice pulls me from my train of thought. "I was thinking you'd never show. Glad to see you. And, you brought someone with you." Chase puts both hands on the bar and leans in. After ogling Gretchen, he turns his cocky grin on me. "Hey, I'm Chase. I'm guessing you know nothing about me from our girl Gretchen here."

Chase is amusing. But even more so is how tense Gretchen gets next to me. She rarely gets flustered or bothered—but apparently, she does around him. *Hmm...*

"Oh, you are going to be interesting." I smile and stick my hand out for him to shake. "I'm Jules, *our girl Gretchen's* roommate. And I know enough, but what I *didn't*, I learned the moment we walked in this place."

Chase and I both smile at each other, while Gretchen rolls her eyes and groans before putting her head in her hands.

Chase checks us over and gives me a crooked grin, raising one eyebrow. "Oh, Jules, I think you and I are going to get along great. Welcome—both of you—to Portland Social. What can I get you ladies to drink?"

I let Gretchen take the lead on this, unsure what she wants to do.

"I think I'll try the Cinnamon Maple Whiskey Sour off your fall menu. She'll have a pinot blanc. Thanks, Chase." The smile she gives him is sincere.

White wine is my go-to when out with others or with someone I'm not comfortable with yet. It's easy to sip, and others rarely notice if I don't finish or leave my glass somewhere, feigning forgetfulness. I don't like the loss of control alcohol gives. I wasn't sure if Gretchen would order a drink tonight. Usually, she doesn't. Yet she knew without asking that I'd take a white wine.

"Coming right up, lad—" He doesn't finish his sentence and

suddenly yells across the room. "Man, what did I do right today? You didn't tell me you'd be coming in tonight." Chase walks around the bar and behind us, heading toward someone without filling our drink order.

I pivot and glance over my shoulder to see the person Chase is welcoming. And damn am I glad I have one hand on the bar. The guy Chase is talking to is stop-everything-and-look-at-me gorgeous. Brown hair with a bit of a curl to it, at least when it's as wet as it is now—I'm guessing from the rain. He has deep-set eyes. I can't see the color from this far away. His sideburns are longer than most, almost to the tip of his earlobe, and he has light scruff. It's attractive as hell on him. Not to mention his perfectly tailored suit covering what looks like a well-cared-for body. *Damn, he is hot.*

As Chase walks around and gives Mr. Handsome a hug, both slapping each other on the back, I flick my glance to Gretchen and lean in. "Who do you think he is? A brother?"

They're standing over by the entrance and the place is noisy, so I know they can't hear us over at the bar. Yet, we both still gossip in hushed tones.

"Nah, Chase has two older brothers. But I've met them, and that...that is not either of them. Holy hell. He's hot in a boss-me-around-and-have-your-way-with-me kind of way."

"So, Chase..."

"What?"

"Don't *what* me, lady. I've seen you two together for under five minutes and it's obvious there's something deeper to the story you tried to sell me."

Gretchen gazes at Chase over my shoulder, takes a deep exhale, then looks me in the eye. "There is a story. But it isn't a happily ever after ending, so I don't want to recite it to you right now, okay?"

"Okay. I'll drop it. Plus, knowing you trust him is huge. It's enough for now."

"What? Why do you say I trust him?" She spins her ring around her finger.

I turn my entire body to her. "You don't order drinks that often, but you did from Chase. And when he left without filling our drink order to greet his hot friend over there," I tilt my head toward where Chase and his friend are standing, "and the other bartender walked over to finish up, I saw you shake your head no at him. So, at the very least, it's clear you trust him. I'm glad for that."

Gretchen confided in me one night that she was roofied once in college. Ever since, she's been particular with accepting drinks. She didn't even hesitate for Chase to serve her, though. For *her*, that means something.

She just purses her lips and nods at me. It's glaringly obvious she's done with the Chase subject. I'll let it go for now, but we *will* talk about the alluring bar owner later.

While studying Mr. Handsome but still talking to Gretchen, I bite down on my lip. "I might not have wanted to come out tonight, but man am I glad we did." I flick my glance to her, and we both bust out laughing.

"I bet you are."

As we laugh, my cell vibrates. I pull it from my clutch and groan. "I am twenty-four, right?" My question oozes sarcasm with a hint of irritation.

"Uh oh."

I hold up my phone for her to see.

**Eric**: I saw your mom. She said she hasn't heard from you in a week. Don't make her stress. Call her. I hope you're being smart, and home in bed resting after a long week. When do I get to see you next?

I shove my phone back in my purse.

"Stop it." Gretchen places her hand over mine.

"Stop what?"

"Playing with your worry bracelet. Forget the meddling mom

and the hot-for-you hometown cop. It's Friday night, and you can make of it what you will. So, where do you want it to go?"

*Where do I want it to go…?*

I peer back over to the sexy stranger Chase is still talking to, considering this.

2

## HUNTER

"*M*an, what did I do right today? You didn't tell me you'd be coming in tonight," I hear Chase yell across the room as I walk farther into Portland Social. He comes up to me, and we both throw an arm around each other.

This bar is Chase's baby. Even when we were brothers in our fraternity, he talked about opening a place like Portland Social. And here it is.

Like others with good ideas but not enough money behind them, he didn't know who or where to turn to. But Chase has been there for me like no one else. So, for me, there wasn't a second thought to put up the money for him. He had issues with the idea, the whole mixing-business-and-friendship thing. Maybe since money is still new to me, I didn't have those issues. I told him he could think of me as an investor. As I told him though, to me, this is all his.

I haven't made time in the weeks since he's opened to come in. I missed the grand opening because I was busy in China and couldn't make it back. Things at work have been chaos over the last eight months.

The space is astounding as I take it all in. The crowd is an eclectic mixture of Portland. Over in the corner are some dart-boards, which I believe he probably put in for me. It only makes me feel like shit yet again, that I haven't made stopping by more of a priority. When we talked about him opening a place, we both said how great it would be to have a base for us to catch up. He built it, and I haven't come.

Next to the dartboards are two pool tables, both in use. The bar is massive and packed. Most people are paired up, except for one guy at the end whose body language even from here screams, *"I just want to be alone."*

I'm in awe. He did it. He created the perfect place to meet up, to start or end a night in. I push all thoughts of Chase to the side though when my gaze finds *her.*

It's like I've hit my target. As I follow the sensual-as-hell legs up to the most perfect ass, my breath hitches. I can only see half of her face as she turns toward the girl on her right. Her blonde hair flows freely just below her shoulder blades in soft curls. The curls almost form an arrow to that stunning ass.

"See something you like, asshole?" Chase leans in and whispers, breaking my trance.

"What are you talking about?" I rub my hand on the back of my neck. *Shit, have I been that obvious in checking out that girl? Who can blame me? Who wouldn't look at her?*

"Oh, please. I see you eye-fucking my customer."

"Same Chase." I shake my head. Glancing again to the blonde over Chase's shoulder, I jut my chin out. "Do you know her?"

"Ha. Same Hunter, always to the point. Honestly, I don't. I just met her. She's the roommate of an old friend."

I eventually turn my attention to him. "God, you've done it. This is amazing."

"Amazing, huh? You talking about our bar or the girl? Because you seem like you're spending a lot of time looking at one in particular, and I know how precious your time is."

I cringe. He said nothing directed at my absence, but I heard the disappointment in his voice. Chase is a loyal friend. He's worked his butt off for this place. I let him down, giving money but no time to this project.

"First, it's *your* bar. Second, I am sorry, man. There's no excuse for not getting here sooner, so I won't waste your time trying to come up with one. But seriously, this place is awesome. Well done, brother." I place my hand on his shoulder and take another look around.

"Thanks. That means more than I can say. Especially coming from you, Hunter. Now, how about you come up to the bar, and I'll get you a drink and maybe introduce you to that beautiful blonde?"

I can't even play it cool because the words are out before I can even think. "Introduce us? Hell, please tell me you haven't slept with her."

"Dude," he shakes his head, laughing at me, "I told you, I just met her. Even I'm not that talented. Come on, stop acting so nervous. It's creeping me out seeing you like this. Bring back my in-control, cocky ass of a friend."

We both laugh, then Chase walks ahead of me to my blonde mystery and says something to her and her friend. He leads as they follow him down to where a group is settling their tab and pulling coats on.

I quickly follow as the two women take their seats, and I snag the empty one next to my girl with the blonde hair, though I don't sit yet. She gives me an odd look.

"Musical chairs. I didn't want to be left without." I smile, but it's an awkward one, probably too many teeth showing. I try to stop, but it's like it's frozen on my face.

With her eyes wide and her eyebrows raised, she turns her attention to her friend.

*Musical chairs? What the hell?* I don't even understand what I'm talking about.

Chase stands near the table while chuckling, presumably at me. At least I'm providing him some comedic relief. "Ladies, I apologize about your drinks," he says. "I'll make them now. And Hunter, what can I get you?"

"Old-fashioned, please."

After he goes off to fill our drink orders, I sit there trying to figure out how to talk to her.

"So, drinks on a Friday night, huh? Celebrating or commiserating? The rain. It's Friday night. Does the sky not appreciate that?" I rub the back of my neck.

*What the fuck is wrong with me?* I do not have these problems. Meeting and conversing with women is usually easy for me, but I'm nervous as hell. I run my fingers through my damp hair.

"Here's your drink, man. Ah, where are my manners? Hunter, this here is my friend Gretchen. And, I'm sorry, love, I get so many names a night I don't recall yours."

Bless the ground he walks on. I give Chase a lopsided grin and subsequently come face to face with her. I put my hand out for introductions. My gaze is never off her face.

She doesn't take my hand, but ultimately, she speaks. "Hi, I'm Jules."

# 3
## JULES

*hy is he sitting with us?* I gawk at Gretchen, but all she does is shrug.

Chase had come up to us saying he could get us a table, so I didn't have to stand anymore. His hot friend followed like a lost puppy. A confused, lost puppy who apparently doesn't know how to speak coherently.

"Hunter."

Gretchen kicks me under the table, and I glare at her. She nods her head over to the awkward stranger, and I see he has his hand out.

"What?" I ask, with just my left eyebrow raised.

She nods her head toward the lost puppy again.

He laughs nervously, drawing my attention. "My name— Hunter. It's my name. Nice to meet you."

I glance down at his hand again.

Taking a deep breath and forcing a smile, I place my hand in his for an intended quick shake. But the second our skin touches, my lungs nearly stop working. My gaze meets his, and in that moment, it's obvious he feels it too. His eyes almost look as if they're pulsing. There's an instant electric charge between us. I quickly lick my lips, and his glance momentarily follows, our hands still clasped.

"Awkward," Gretchen singsongs as she breaks our hands apart. "And not that you want to chat with me, Hunter, but that's too bad. My grandma raised me with manners. I'm Gretchen, Gretchen Holt."

She takes his hand, and their connection lasts a few seconds. I watch his reaction the whole time, but it's obvious there's no charge with her.

"Nice to meet you, Ms. Holt," Hunter says.

"Oh, please, I'm not at work. It's Gretchen. What do you do, Hunter?" she asks.

Chase laughs. "This should be entertaining. Enjoy getting to know one another. Too bad I'm off to run a business. Just holler if you need refills." He leaves us at our table to fend for ourselves.

My breathing thankfully returned to normal once Gretchen broke the physical connection between me and Hunter. With his eyes still on me, I look to Gretchen quickly then back to him, smirking. I tilt my head toward Gretchen to clue Hunter in that he's possibly being rude. Even though I'd take all his attention if I could, I don't want Gretchen to be ignored.

Hunter takes my hint and clears his throat. He turns his body toward Gretchen. "Sorry, I missed what you said. Could you repeat it, please?"

"Shocking," she says jokingly, while placing her hand on her chest. "I asked what you do for work. You are employed, aren't you?"

He laughs and finally seems to relax a bit. He turns on his stool to focus a bit on Gretchen but keeps giving me glances. "Yes, I'm employed. I run an investment firm. What is it you ladies do—assuming you are employed?" He says it in a teasing tone, and I like that he isn't too serious.

Gretchen doesn't speak at first, like she's waiting to see if I will. Instead, I skip my wine and grab one of the waters Chase had placed for us on the center of our table. I can't talk yet, because I don't want to. I don't feel calm, I feel discombobulated, and I don't do flustered. I like to be in control of my surroundings, and, most importantly, myself.

"We're both teachers. I teach first grade and Jules here," Gretchen points to me and his attention follows, "teaches kindergarten."

He turns to me. "Kindergarten? That's remarkable. I have so much respect for teachers. Is your school nearby?"

Finally finding my voice, I reply, "Yes, it's just down the street. Boise-Eliot Humboldt Elementary."

"Ah, a Title One school. Even more respect to you ladies. Drinks are on me tonight."

"How did you know our school is Title One?" I ask.

"My firm donates often to the local schools. I've made it a point to familiarize myself with which ones are most in need in our community." He shrugs, as if it's no big deal.

It is to me, though. My students are everything to me; that school is my second home. We pour all we can into it.

"It's a beautiful building. However, it's an ancient building. I bet you face a lot of challenges there," he says.

He isn't wrong. They built it in 1926. I love the school, but I envy the brand-new schools built out in the suburbs with everything shiny and pristine. "We make it work. The community is phenomenal."

"You must really love what you do. You smile when you talk about it, and I can tell it's genuine. You probably don't even realize you're doing it."

He speaks of my job with such reverence. Most people hear *teacher* and make some crack about how they'd love to only have to work for nine months and get off at two every workday. It's in my contract to be at work until 3:10, but I'm usually there later because of how much I love my job. His admiration, I find affirming.

I turn my knees a bit toward him before saying anything else, but in the process, I knock my purse. Before I can hop off the stool to retrieve it, Hunter does. As he bends, his right hand grazes my inner right calf and travels down to my ankle. My skin is instantly covered in goosebumps, and my breathing becomes erratic. Why does this guy affect me so much? Furthermore, why do I like the way it feels?

He gazes at me. I'm sure he can see the reaction my body has to his touch. My cheeks heat, and he smiles at me, making me blush even more.

"Here you go." Hunter hands my purse to me, his eyes darker than before. The way he looks at me makes me want to strip him of all his clothes. I don't hide the fact that I slowly inspect every inch of his tall stature.

"What exactly is an investment firm?" I ask, trying to sound casual.

"In the simplest form, it's pooled money that's invested to buy shares or other assets."

I take in his appearance, and it's obvious from what he has on that, at the very least, he dresses as if he's successful. "Impressive, especially for someone your age."

"Ah, yes, I am very fortunate. My adoptive father started the firm decades ago. Don't get me wrong, I've earned every promotion. But I'm afraid nepotism played a part in me taking it over when Benjamin passed away not too long ago."

I place my hand over his. "I'm sorry to hear that. Were you close?"

He glances off to the side as if trying to weigh his response. "I was very lucky Benjamin took me in. He was always more like a mentor than a parent to me, but I appreciate the life he gave me."

He's so open with his answers. I find his honesty beautiful

and confounding. We sit there, just looking at each other, my hand still over his. His thumb moves back and forth on my palm, and the contact is comforting.

"Oh my gosh. I have no idea what's going on, but you two are making me feel like a voyeur. So, I'm off to use the restroom. While I'm gone, you two can chat, or…leave to go screw this tension out of your systems. But do *something* before I return so this awkwardness can be over."

I hide my face behind my hand. I forgot Gretchen was sitting right here with us. She always speaks her mind and rarely apologizes for it. She's one of the most genuine people I know. I also know, out of the options she stated, which I'd like to do.

"Your friend isn't subtle, is she?" Hunter's voice is deep and sensual.

"Gretchen? No. She doesn't believe in wasting any time being indirect."

"And you? Do you waste time?"

My eyes widen with the question. I try to think of a fun and flirty answer, but I'm not good with being overly girly. I'm not a giggler or someone who fawns over a guy. "I'm usually pretty good with the use of my time."

He looks away, picks up a spare coaster. I watch him tap it on the table as he spins it. He lets out a slow breath. "Well, I'm one that also likes to be direct. Is it okay if I speak candidly?"

"I'd appreciate that."

He smiles at me again. *God, I love his smile.* "I think you can feel this connection between us—it's insane," he says, to which I nod. "I won't speak for you, but for me, *this*," he motions between us, "isn't normal."

I give a slight shake of my head to let him know this isn't normal for me either.

"So, I'd like to take you out. Maybe tomorrow or the next night? I know it's sudden, but I fly out soon for work, and I don't want more time to pass than has to…"

"Ye—wait, what? A date? You don't want to get out of here now? Together?" I was so excited to leave, to feel his hands on me, that I caught what he was asking as if it were on a five-second time delay.

"Trust me, all those thoughts you're having, I am too." He leans in closer to me. "But I don't want just a night with you, no matter how mind-blowing it might be. As I said, this kind of...*connection* is new for me, and I want to treat it—and you—special. Let me take you out, Jules. What do you say?" He smiles at me, and it's like I can see the confidence coming off him in waves. He knows I'm interested in him. He thinks he has me.

My excitement over meeting him deflates. I don't date.

"Sorry, Hunter, I'm not interested in a date." I hop off the stool and gather my purse.

He places his hand on my arm, and again, instantly, my body responds to the contact. *Traitor.*

"Wait, did I miss something? Did I offend you?" His aura of certainty is gone as he searches my eyes for an explanation.

"No worries, you didn't offend me. I just don't date. If you're interested in enjoying each other's company tonight, I'm game, but that's all I'm looking for. It was nice meeting you, Hunter."

"You're serious?"

"Yes." I start walking away. But for the first time, I second-guess my decision in turning someone down.

"Play me for it." His voice booms over the others around us.

Turning, I purse my lips while I repeat his statement in my head, trying to figure out his angle. He takes this time to walk over to me.

"What are you talking about?" I ask him.

"Your idea, really. You said you were game for it. So, play me. If you win, we leave together tonight, have an incredible evening we'll probably fondly remember for the rest of our lives, and never see each other again. If I win, I get a date with you. One I plan and pick you up for."

I go to interrupt him, but he puts a finger up, halting me.

"I can see the fear. Calm down. I said I'll plan it because something tells me you're used to being in control. I'd like to show you that you can give some of that up and still have a fun evening. And I want to pick you up because I'm a gentleman." He smiles down at me, and I break and smile back. "You are special, Jules, and you deserve to be treated as such. I just want to spend time with you. That's all. Promise."

I smirk, while amusement dances in his eyes. "First, I said I was game for leaving with you tonight. And I don't want to go on a date, as I have clearly stated, so why would I agree to this?"

He steps in and places his right hand on my lower back. As he looks into my eyes, I have to clench my thighs together from the instant ache I feel. *God, what would it be like if we slept together?*

"You only have to worry if you plan on losing. And something tells me you don't do things to lose."

"You're right. I don't like to lose." I take a moment to make it seem like I'm mulling it over, but I know I'm going to say yes —only, on my terms. "Fine. I'm game. However, I get to pick what we play."

"Fine by me. Lady's choice." He turns to the side, moving his left hand, palm up like a display worker.

I should feel surer, but somehow, it's like I just stepped into the lion's den. Especially with the smug grin he's giving me.

"Darts," I say, without even bothering to turn away. I spotted the dartboards when Gretchen and I walked in.

"You say that with a lot of conviction, Jules." He smiles at me as he skims my skin with his right thumb where my skirt and sweater meet.

My heart races. He's right; I feel confident with darts. My parents had a dartboard that hung on the wall between my room and the bathroom Mitch and I shared. Every night, we played a game of darts before getting ready for bed.

The last year Mitch was alive, I finally had grown into my

body. I was stronger. Not stronger than him, but still, my accuracy improved to where I won more than I lost against my brother.

"When I win, we leave right away and head to your place," I tell him.

"Why mine?"

"Something tells me, with you, I won't be very quiet," I admit, and he makes a noise that sounds like a low growl. "I don't want to keep Gretchen awake."

His gaze turns molten as it drops to my lips. He wants to kiss me. I'm sure of it. I slowly wet my lips, enjoying the attention he pays to this.

"You are very considerate. Just to let you know, I have never wanted to win something more in my entire life."

"What?" I ask, unable to hide my shock.

"I told you, Jules. I want you, but I want more than one night. I want to win and show you why."

We hear someone clear their throat near us. I finally step back, and he allows me to without a fight. I spot Gretchen and Chase standing to my left, watching us.

"See, I told you they looked like they were going to have sex in your bar. I'd watch them if I were you," Gretchen teases Chase.

"You two, keep it classy. I'm not about to have the police called because you can't keep it together." Chase walks away, shaking his head.

I'm sure we come off like horny teenagers to him. "I have to use the restroom. How about you get the darts from Chase or one of the other bartenders? Maybe you can warm up with Gretchen."

"Warm up? For what?" Gretchen questions.

I walk away without answering; Hunter can fill her in. I need a few moments to rein in my emotions. I stay hidden in the back corner by the hallway leading to the restrooms and watch as he warms up. Weird, I know. But I need to steady myself, and saying I had to use the restroom was an easy excuse. Hunter wasn't in the plan for tonight. He shouldn't be in the plan for any night.

Yet, I haven't had this much fun bantering with a guy in...*Lord*, I can't remember when. Most guys I've spent time with since graduating high school I'd describe as self-absorbed. People focused on themselves are easily distracted with questions about themselves when I don't want to talk about me. They've been attractive too, but not striking. Someone with distractingly good looks usually has too much confidence.

People like Hunter. He is beautiful. That isn't a term most men would want to be called. But seriously, watching him from this dark hallway, it's the first word that comes to me. I don't like this feeling—this flutter inside. I have successfully avoided flutters, goosebumps, shivers, and flickers of any kind. Until tonight. *Damn him.*

I watch as Hunter rolls his sleeves up almost to his elbows before his first turn against Gretchen. The way his forearm ripples does something inside me. *When did I start finding forearms sexy?* I take a breath as he wraps his fingers around the dart and rotates his hand a few times down at his side. He brings it up and says something that makes him and Gretchen both laugh. I wish I could have heard it. His laughter is easy and unrestrained.

I suck in a couple of breaths, mentally slap myself across the face, and slip on my armor before making my way back over to him. I can't let him distract me again. Because I already know, if I'm not prepared, he'll worm his way in. Not only is Hunter better-looking than any guy I've spent time with, I'm also not used to how direct of a person he is. He's been crystal clear with what he wants. What's irritating is how comfortable he makes me, all while unnerving me with his honesty. Someone so open and sure of himself. *Deep breath. I can do this.*

"All right, showtime. It's me and you," I say as I join them.

"Oh, I like the way that sounds." Hunter gives an easy smile, and I'm pretty sure I can't hide the grin I give back. *Damn.*

I roll my eyes at him. "Darts, Hunter. Darts."

"First, can I grab you another drink? I think you left yours at the table, and it got bussed already."

"Nah, I'm good, but thank you." I grab the darts from his open palm, my fingertips just grazing his. They're so warm, and I'm sure he hears my intake of breath. My eyes look to his, and by the darkening of his gaze, he detects the same sparks.

Trying to expand my lungs from the sudden lack of air, I taunt him. "Just to warn you, I have skills. Skills that would impress most. But since you made this personal, I will not impress you. I will just decimate you."

"Decimate? Damn. That's a powerful statement. Not that you'd know, but I deal with cutthroat people all day, every day, billions of their dollars in my hands. I handle pressure exceptionally well."

"Cutthroat business, huh? Trying to impress me?"

"Nope. Just stating a fact." He motions with his hand for me to go first.

Bringing my hand around eye level, I line up where I hope to make my mark. I take a slight inhale and pitch the dart forward, letting go. It sails smoothly through the air, the arrow hitting the center green. I raise my arms in triumph and do a little shimmy.

"Proud of yourself?" Hunter asks, laughing. He takes in my victory dance, not hiding his enjoyment of my hip shake.

The heat radiates in my cheeks as they redden. He breaks our stare, walks up, and lines his body up for his turn. Being slightly behind him has its advantages. It's obvious he takes pride in himself, in how fine his suit pants hang and how his shoulders ripple under his white dress shirt. He tosses his tie over his shoulder so it won't be in his way, looking at me as he does so and giving me a grin that just makes me want his mouth on mine.

"Stop stalling and throw," Gretchen yells, watching our spectacle from the side.

His shot is good. Not as beneficial as mine though, and I'm hopeful about my odds.

By the time we each have one last throw, I'm currently ahead. I step into place and try to calm my breath. Just one more shot and this evening ends how I want. *No big deal.* As I line up, I feel air by my left ear and warmth at my back.

"Don't be nervous. I promise I will take superb care of you on our date." Hunter softly states each word by my ear so only I can hear.

Instantly, my nipples harden. *Screw him and his sex appeal.* I need to snap out of this Hunter fog and control the narrative better. It's been a fun night, but it needs to be left at that.

I ignore his words and give no reply aside from my perfect throw. Well, it would have been perfect, if at the last second before the dart left my hand Hunter's hand hadn't slowly skimmed my hip, making me inhale a sharp breath. It isn't a bad score, but it isn't what I aimed for. *Shit.*

I glare at him, trying to formulate a revenge plan. I deal with five and six-year-olds who tattle on and copycat one another all day. *Hmm. Copycat.* Perfect. I'll just do exactly what he did. So, I resort to seducing him to throw him off his game. I'm not proud of it, but desperate times call for sometimes using efficient but questionable tactics.

As he lines up, instead of stepping behind him, I go to his periphery and move my sweater a bit more off my shoulder, showing off the upper mound of my breast. I stand there and bite my bottom lip. He immediately turns his view fully on me. Mission accomplished. But then, while looking directly at me, he shoots his last dart and hits red, dead center. Bullseye.

He walks over and pulls my lip down to remove it from my

teeth, then strokes my lip gently with the pad of his thumb before removing his hand. "Thank you for the incentive there at the end. I thought you had it—and if you didn't remind me what I was fighting for, you probably would have. But, since I won, what night this week works for you?"

"What night works for me? For what?"

"Our date. I'm the victor, and to me come the spoils."

I laugh. I laugh so hard at that—at him. "Is that supposed to do something for me?"

"A bet is a bet. This coming week too, because I don't want to wait to see you again. And as I mentioned, I leave soon for a business trip."

*This* is a problem.

*Hunter* is a problem, a threat to my orderly life. I have to make sure this is our one and *only* date—and quickly. "Tomorrow."

"Tomorrow?" He smirks at me. "Excellent. Good to see you're in just as big of a rush to see me again as I am you."

*I'm in trouble.*

# 4

## HUNTER

"Scare her off already?" Chase asks, glancing up from his desk as I enter his office.

"Ass," I scoff. "One of your bartenders said you were back here. Is it okay if I come in? And no, I didn't scare her away."

"I wouldn't have this place at all if it weren't for your investment, so you never have to ask to come back here." He looks me over and shakes his head while smiling. "The instant you walked in and saw Jules tonight, I knew that girl had you all twisted up. Your body language changed completely. For someone who's usually unflappable, you were stumbling over your words like a nervous kid at his first dance. It was awesome to watch. You're screwed. Fire in your hands, man. Fire in your hands."

I mull this over. "If I wanted to get screwed, I would have left with her. She offered. But did you see her?" I drag my hand down my face and around the back of my neck to rub it. "She is not someone you enjoy just an evening with and then let slip away."

"You met her, let's see," he glances at his phone to check the time, "four and a half hours ago and you're already talking longevity. What's up? This isn't you." He shoves the keyboard away from him, places his elbows on the desk, and takes a deep breath. "I haven't seen you in a while. Are you sure you're handling everything okay?"

He's right; I'm not rash or careless. But this has nothing to do with the added stress of my new position. Or the loss of Benjamin. I might have inherited Steeple Investments, but Benjamin wouldn't have left it to me if I hadn't earned it. I have a reputation for deliberate behavior. Tonight, I was not at my finest.

"I appreciate the concern, man. Seriously. You're the only one that checks in on me. But I promise I'm good. I won't lie and say the firm isn't a lot, but I got it. I learned from the best."

"How are things with Benjamin's estate? Any issues or is everything a done deal?"

"Other than what he bequeathed to charities, I inherited. I didn't have to fight anyone over anything, so that was nice. But having a billion dollars in assets suddenly handed to you tends to have people coming from every direction with their hands out. Nothing I can't handle, though."

I look over and see a picture on a floating shelf on the wall of the two of us. I can't place it, though it has to be from my sophomore or junior year. It strikes me how young we appear. We're both dressed in button-down shirts and ties. It had to have been from one of our fraternity events.

I met Chase my sophomore year when he pledged the fraternity I was a member of. I ended up being his big brother. Now he is the person closest to me.

The fact that Chase has a photo of us in his office stirs something inside me. He's the closest thing to family I have left. It means a lot with how large and incredible his family is that he still values our relationship as much as I do.

"That was a fun night," Chase says, standing and coming over to me when he notices the photo I'm looking at.

"I don't remember what it's from."

"It was my freshman year, so your sophomore. It's from our fraternity's formal dance. Seems forever ago, doesn't it?"

I nod and look up to the ceiling, trying to think. "I honestly can't even remember who I took."

"I went with Carrie something. She was a freshman. I think you went with one of her sorority sisters."

I turn toward him and for a moment I weigh asking my next question, but curiosity wins. "Did you ever take Gretchen to one of our formals? I don't remember her."

Chase steps back. "Gretchen? Why would you ask that?"

"She said something about knowing you back then, when we were playing darts. Talking about you seemed to make her nervous. But she said you guys are old friends."

"Yeah, we went to the same high school. Actually, she went to Oregon University with us, but she wasn't in our scene, so I'm not surprised you don't remember her. And no, I never took her to a formal."

He doesn't say more and doesn't look as though he wants to, so I leave it at that.

I'm not surprised I don't remember my date. I've dated plenty but haven't seriously dated anyone. My actual parents were no model of what a solid, healthy relationship might look like. And Benjamin didn't date, at least as far as I knew. I've been around Chase's family plenty. I've seen the love his parents have for each other; it's palpable. I want that. I just don't know how to find it.

Tonight, though...the second I saw Jules, things just started clicking. When we touched, it was the first time I ever physically felt a spark. I know how to treat a lady, and I have cared if the women I'm with are happy or upset. But this *need*, to see her happy, is new. When she laughed tonight, I couldn't help but watch. It felt like, in the cacophony of the room, her laughter was all I heard.

"There's just something about this girl," I muse aloud,

changing the subject. "I can't even put it into words. But I need to know more. I need to be around her. And while I appreciate your concern, I told you, I'm good. Benjamin's passing was a surprise. Finding out he left me his firm was an even bigger shock. But I'm handling it all, I promise."

Chase looks me over like he's trying to decide if I'm being honest enough about my feelings. I know he worries. I had little time to mourn Benjamin's sudden passing. It felt like the second I was notified of his heart attack, I was then ushered into my new role in what was *his* company. Some weren't thrilled with my succession, but I'm trying my best to prove myself.

"There's no reason to worry, Chase. I know I acted out of character tonight. But at the same time, when can you honestly say I've ever held back when wanting something?" I smirk even though in truth, I'm scared. One shot, and I may lose her.

He shakes his head with a slight laugh. "Dude, you aren't someone to waste time, so if you want to chase after her, just know you *will* be chasing. She's not someone that gives off let's-live-happily-ever-after vibes. I just don't want to see you hurt."

I let his words roll around for a minute. As my best friend, I know he has my best interest at heart.

"What's the plan, then?" he asks. "You always have one. So, when it comes to Miss Jules, what's on the agenda?"

"We're going out tomorrow. She's giving me one chance, and I have to make it perfect."

"Tomorrow?"

"Maybe she's as eager as I am." I smile at him with confidence.

"Eager or looking to just get it over with?" he counters.

I want to contradict him, but I can't. I thought the same. But regardless of her motives, I have my own. I have an opportunity to convince her that life is too short to toss the connection and chemistry we have to the side.

I turn back and take in the rest of the photos he's picked to have in his office. My stomach twists in a familiar ache when it comes to Chase and his family—jealousy. I love him like a brother, and he's always treated me as such. But they raised him with a full support system. And those people are displayed here in his space. I'm honored to be among them. But I try not to read into the fact that my photo is on its own shelf with some decorative item, while the other three shelves are filled with photos of him with his actual family.

I'm an only child. As much as I wish I had an ally those formative years, I'm glad no one else had to suffer at my father's hands other than me and my mother. He was a mean son of a bitch.

My earliest memory is of making him a drawing. I had used a brown paper bag my mom used to pack my dad's lunch in. I remember grabbing one of the pens from my mom's drawer. I didn't have crayons or anything like that growing up. My dad said that stuff was a waste of money. I drew a picture of me and him hunting, even though he never once took me with him. Maybe I wished he would, or that my drawing would spur him to bring me along the next time.

Who knows what the mind of a four-year-old thinks? When I showed him, he smacked me so hard across the face I got knocked down and landed on my side. He said I wasted a perfectly good lunch sack. Then, he crumpled up my drawing and threw it on the floor next to me. I don't know if that was the first time he hit me. I doubt it. It's just the first time I remember.

I learned young that no matter how good or nice you are, you can't control someone else's mood. Trust me, I tried. But it taught me how to adapt—easily.

"You okay? You seem lost." Chase places his hand on my shoulder.

I rub my cheek, like the memory also brought back the pain. I pull my phone from my pocket and show Chase the screen.

"Just work. I could feel all the notifications going off in my pocket," I lie.

Chase has gathered a lot of pieces of my childhood that I've given him through the years. But not all memories need to be shared.

"Any idea what you'll do for your date?" Chase asks as he heads back around his desk to sit.

"I have an idea. And if it works...I should be golden."

# 5

## JULES

*ick?* No, too basic.

*Need to stay in and work?* Even I know that's a weak lie.

I could just say I have an emergency. *Ugh.* I need to get out of this date. Why did I agree to the bet to begin with? This wasn't wise. Meeting Hunter has totally thrown me off. Last night was supposed to be about Gretchen. I'm a shitty friend. *Oh.* I could cancel to stay with Gretchen. *Sorry, my roommate needs me.* Perfect.

"No. You are not lying your way out of this date."

*Shit, I must have said that last one out loud.* I groan. "Why not? I don't want to go. It isn't a big deal. I mean, when will I cross paths with him again? He said so himself, he's leaving soon for a business trip. Who cares if I burn a bridge?"

"*Why not?*" she mimics. "Because I can't remember the last date, or heck, forget date—I can't even remember the last hookup you had. Even our seventy-two-year-old neighbor across the hall gets more action than you do."

"Eww. Please don't make me picture Mrs. Johnson like that."

"All I'm saying is, hon, if Mrs. Johnson is giving it up more than you...it's time to look inward." She pokes me in the chest.

BETTER DAYS | 47

I pick up the pillow next to her and toss it at her. Though, sadly, she's right. It has been a while. Gosh, when was the last time...*January, I think?* No, it had to have been before Christmas. Scott was his name. Or Chris. *Nope.* It was Derrick. *Yes.* He worked for a marketing firm downtown and kept trying to impress me by name-dropping the athletes and singers he represented and the gossip he knew. "Ha. Derrick was the last guy."

"So, you remember his name. Do you want a prize?" She slow claps. *Bitch.* She actually slow claps for me. I just glare at her as she continues. "The point being how long it's been, not so much who it was with."

"Fine, it's been a beat since I was last with someone. That doesn't make me desperate."

"So, what was wrong with him? Derrick. I didn't meet him. In fact, you don't introduce anyone to me. I can think of *one* time I got home late and some guy was in the kitchen, sans clothes, getting a glass of water. You always say something's wrong with them. Is it Eric?"

"Is what Eric?"

"Who you're waiting for?" She laughs. She knows it isn't him; she hears me whine enough when I get his overbearing texts or calls.

"Ew, brat." I whack her with the pillow. "Anyway...moving on. I am not waiting for anyone. Why would you even bring him up?"

"Do you remember our first week in the apartment? You didn't respond to your mom's texts and didn't return her phone calls for two days, so Eric drove up to check on you. Oh my gosh, your face when he showed up was priceless."

"Ugh, I try to forget my mom's overbearing moments. It was nice of him to drive up for her, but yeah, he doesn't deter any of her tendencies."

For weeks after the funerals, I avoided Eric. It wasn't fair to him. But with him being Matt's brother, it was too hard to see him. We were friends because our families hung out.

However, while he thought we could become closer and bond over losing our brothers, I wanted to scream at him that I loved his brother. I wanted to scream that I'd had a crush on Matt since I met him the first time he came over to my house. That my silly, schoolgirl self had pictured marrying him one day. That I thought I'd get my teaching credential and teach in our small town while Matt would follow his dream into the police academy. And that whenever I pictured having a family, it was always with Matt by my side.

But I didn't. Instead, everything stayed locked inside where I stuffed it down and kept it. It gave me a sense of control. I felt too guilty over Matt to talk about him with anyone else.

He was in that car at that moment because of me. Mitch always took him home after practice. But that night he wanted to come over, probably because of us having sex earlier. He wouldn't have been in the car if he wasn't coming to see me. It was my fault, and my punishment to suffer alone.

Eric decided to go for his brother's dream and entered the police academy. I stuck with my teaching path, but I didn't want to be in Redmond anymore. So, I filed Matt away into a folder of my past. I promised myself I'd never let anyone else get that close. When you genuinely let people in, you surrender control. You give life the ability to ruin your heart, whether it's on purpose or just part of loving someone.

I look through Gretchen's clothes to see if I can find something to wear tonight since she won't let me flake. "Why are we talking about all of this again?"

"Mostly to make you laugh. And because teasing you about Eric riles you up." She looks down at her hands and takes a deep breath before looking at me again. "But...you're so secretive about your life before Portland. I get this deep, wounded vibe from you. I figure there's someone out there who still owns your heart, and it's why you won't give it to anyone else. So, if it's not Eric, it's someone else. But what was wrong with Derrick? You didn't give him a chance."

"Derrick was fine. Nothing was wrong with him. Relationships just aren't my thing. And if you entertain a guy more than a couple of times, the point is to move toward a relationship, so I stick with just once."

"One day I'm going to get you to tell me."

"I just told you."

"Not about Derrick. About the guy. The one that battered your heart so badly you've sworn off all other men. I will find him and hurt him." She puts her fist in the air in an angry war-cry motion. "He will feel the wrath of Gretchen." We both laugh.

Laughing with her soothes my soul. We both recognize how ridiculous she sounds. But only I'm aware of how fruitless her mission will be. Matt isn't around to find. I gave him my heart, and I don't think I ever truly got it back, at least not whole. Now it's easier to not even try. So, I don't. I'm sure if I thought about it, I'd realize maybe I'm punishing myself by not allowing myself to talk about him. He's been just mine—my secret—for so long, I don't know if I'll ever share about him. About us. Plus, just thinking about him brings up a lot of guilt.

Trying to lighten the mood, I move the conversation back to my dilemma with Hunter. "Come on, help me. How do I get out of this?" I smile, hoping it'll win her over.

"Nice try. You don't. You put on your big-girl panties. But make them sexy 'cause you just never know." She wiggles her eyebrows. "And you go. And maybe if you're lucky, you'll come later." She falls onto her side, laughing at her own creativity. Gretch often performs for an audience of one.

"Fine, at least help me get ready," I whine.

The next hour consists of outfit selection, makeup, and hair. Gretchen offers me a glass of wine to help calm my nerves, but I decline. I need to be of a rational mind for this date. Something tells me that Hunter is used to getting what he wants, and he's been incredibly clear that what he wants is me. There's just something about him I can't explain or rationalize. I'm scared if I don't keep my walls up, he'll get me. Because maybe part of me wants him to. That scares me the most.

"Jules," Gretchen says, pulling me from my thoughts.

"Yeah?"

"I'm going to wait in the front room so I can answer the door while you finish up, okay?"

"That works. Thanks." My stomach rolls with unease, and maybe a smidge of excitement.

I haven't been on a proper date. Ever. Matt and I never got to that point. Other guys, I've always just met somewhere. No one has ever come to my place to pick me up before. It's stupid to be just shy of twenty-five and still this nervous for a date. *Come on, Jules. Control your emotions*, I school myself. I take a deep breath and wait.

I'm ready, but I need some alone time to try to calm myself.

So, I sit on the bed and wait for the knock.

# 6

## HUNTER

*I* do not get nervous in most situations. I can read people easily, and I've always used it to my advantage. It gives me a sense of control, even if it is an illusion.

Losing both my parents at a young age made control—real or perceived—important. I've learned that if you keep too much in or build your walls too high, you end up giving others control. That's why I always try to put it all out there. Lay all my cards out.

I couldn't read Jules last night. I think that was part of her allure. Which is odd when it would usually unnerve me. She, however, intrigued me. But as I head over to her place, a foreign feeling takes root in my stomach. I am nervous. *Shit.* She made me feel this way last night, too. Why do I care so much about her opinion of me?

As I pull up to her apartment, I look around. She told me last night that she and Gretchen live together, in walking distance to Portland Social. It's a great location, near plenty of bars, stores, and restaurants. As I stare up at their building, I do a last mental check to get my head straight.

I look at the panel of names and see there are eight units. I find the one that says **HOLT/MORGAN** and press the call button. Gretchen answers and hits whatever is needed to buzz me in. I take the steps upstairs two at a time and find their apartment off to the left. Three quick knocks and a deep breath later, Gretchen answers their door.

"Come on in. She's just finishing up. Can I get you anything?" She has a glint in her eye that tells me I have my work cut out for me, but I already figured that.

"Any secret intel you can give me to help out a fellow alum?"

"A fellow alum?" she asks, cocking her head to the side.

"Yeah, Chase told me we all went to the same university. I'm sorry to say I don't remember you from back then, though. Chase and I were frat brothers." I expect her to banter with me like she did last night.

Instead, Gretchen's face pales. Before I can question her reaction, Jules walks into the room. All thoughts of Gretchen disappear once my gaze rakes over Jules. I told her to dress casually. She's in ripped jeans, a tight white tank that perfectly showcases her curves, and a caramel cardigan. I can't speak. She is gorgeous. But her smile sets my blood on fire. I never get stunned speechless, but there's something about her that just obliterates all other thoughts.

"Sorry you had to wait. I'm ready now. Shall we go?" Jules asks. Then, she bites her lip, her eyes taking as greedy a look at my body as mine did hers.

I grab the jacket she's going for on the back of the couch. "Allow me." As I help her into her coat, my fingers graze her collarbone. Such a simple touch, but all I can think is *I want more. I want to bury myself in her. I want her warmth to surround me.*

*What is wrong with me? Slow down and get it together.*

Jules walks over to Gretchen and gives her a hug. "Have a good night. And thanks for before."

Gretchen smiles, and I assume a silent conversation is happening that I'm not privy to.

Jules then looks at me. "Let's head out." She doesn't wait for an acknowledgment from me. She rushes out of the apartment with an air of *the sooner we leave, the sooner this is over.*

I love challenges, and she just unknowingly gave me something to focus on tonight other than my nerves. *Thank you, Jules.*

When we get to my truck, I pull open her door. As she climbs in, her perfume hits me. *Honeysuckle.* We used to have honeysuckle growing near the home I grew up in. Without knowing, I take a deep inhale and stand there like an idiot with my eyes closed. I don't have many happy memories of my childhood, but that scent comforts me.

"Hunter? Are you okay?"

"Honeysuckle." I say it like it's an actual answer. When I open my eyes and look at her, she seems as puzzled as one would expect.

"Sorry. You smell extraordinary. You smell like honeysuckle. It just reminded me of something."

"Oh. Well, something favorable, I hope."

I don't give an answer. I just close the door and make my way over to my side.

"Ready for some fun?" I ask, while a huge grin takes over my face and pushes all memories of my childhood to the back where they belong.

"Well, someone wouldn't tell me anything about tonight, so I can't say I'm ready or not when I don't even know what we're doing."

"You seem to me like the kind of person who enjoys a good challenge. And by the smirk and hitch in your breathing, I'd venture to say I guessed correctly. So, as promised, we're going somewhere we can have a whole lot of fun."

I don't tell her more, and to my shock, she doesn't push for more. We make the short drive to our destination.

"Ground Control? What is this?" she asks as she looks at the venue. "Games?" She looks back at me, confused.

"You've never been? It's a gamer's heaven. Wait there." I exit my truck and go around the front to open her door. I give her my hand to help her down, loving the contact.

"Gamers? Sorry, I'm not following." She looks at me skeptically as she steps to the side, and I close her door.

My nerves roar back to life. *Shit*. This was a reach, but I thought it'd be something she'd be up for.

"They have a ton of arcade games, mostly older ones. After our little competition last night, I thought it would be a good idea. Did I totally miss my mark?"

She puts her hand on my forearm. "No, not at all. It sounds great. It's just...look." She points over her shoulder at the building behind her. "It's closed. We can just call it a night and—"

"Whoa, it isn't open for everyone," I say, not letting her finish that statement. "But you're not just anyone, Jules. I called in a favor. The owner owed me one. The place is open tonight, but only for us."

"'Wow. Um, Hunter, that is sweet, but a bit crazy." She looks at me, her eyes big.

"What are you talking about?"

"You bought out the venue. That's a bit much," she says.

"First, I didn't buy it out for the night. The owner is a friend. They just did a major remodel and haven't reopened yet. Earlier today they had a small thing trying out the new menu and games. I asked my buddy if I could pay him for the staff to stay on for us." I look away for a moment, trying to focus myself. "You didn't want to come tonight." It isn't a question.

Now it's her turn to look away, and she looks down, almost embarrassed.

"The bet was my idea," I continue. "Honestly, I would have asked you out last night without a bet. But you said you don't date. It didn't leave me with a lot of options. I just needed an avenue to get you to go out with me. I had to think fast."

"Do you always say whatever you're thinking?" she asks. "It's unsettling."

"Life is too short to beat around the bush. It's best to be direct. Everyone in my life knows exactly where they stand."

"Wow." She looks at me, and for a moment, I think she's impressed.

*With me? With the venue?* I'm not sure, but I'll take it. "You said that already," I say, with a grin taking up my entire face. I'm trying to keep cool, but making her smile does something to me. I want to make her happy for as long as she'll let me, in whatever way she'll allow.

She purses her lips while looking me over. "I'm trying to decide if it's the smoothest move any guy has ever pulled for me, or if you're trying too hard. You seem earnest, so I'm inclined to think this is...amazing," she finishes, as she turns back to the building and looks at my reflection through the window. She starts to almost vibrate with excitement.

It's either that or nerves. *Shit. I can't tell.*

"I say we go in, order a bunch of appetizers and whatnot, and have some fun playing games. When was the last time you played a bunch of arcade games?" I reach my hand out for her to grasp.

When she takes it, and even gives me a smile, I relax.

The place really is incredible, too. It's such a simple but cool concept. Think of all those times when you were at a pizza place, or bowling alley, or even a movie theater, and begged your parents to let you play just one game. Ground Control is all of that energy with the added benefit of being twenty-one and over so you can enjoy alcohol without kids around. I love watching her take it all in as she looks around once we step inside.

"How about we start with ordering some food and we can eat as we play? Sound good?" I offer.

"Sounds perfect, Hunter."

We go over to where the hostess is and order some small plates to share, drinks, and a large bucket of coins for the games.

She runs her hand down my bicep as we turn to head toward the games, and I love the way her touch feels. "This was a really great idea. I'm looking forward to it."

I start to mentally pat myself on the back until she says more.

"I'm impressed with how confident you are. It's a sexy trait. But just so you're aware, I hate losing. So, be prepared that I'm here to win tonight, and will not be *incentivizing* you like last night." Then she walks away, backward, giving me the cockiest smile and a little laugh that sounds a bit sinister.

"Are you shit talking, Ms.—hell, I don't know your last name."

"Ms. Morgan," she says, giving it freely. "Jules Morgan. And yours?"

"Peterson. Hunter Peterson."

She shakes her head. "I need to watch you. You're too easy to talk to."

"That's a bad thing?"

"Yeah. I think it is."

TWO HOURS later and the place is filled with her laughter. She's laughing without restriction, and it's a fucking turn-on. I need to make her laugh. It becomes like air to me. The sound surrounds me, and I depend on it. Her whole body appears to glow when she laughs. Currently, she's laughing at me, and I don't even mind.

Tears are falling down her cheeks as she tries to gather

enough air to speak. "So." Breath. "What." Breath. "Happened?" Followed by another laughing fit.

"The instructor totally leveled my buddy with a roundhouse kick to his chest. He was flat on his back, and we had to carry him out. I mean, he was an idiot to run into the studio. What the hell did he expect?"

The memory of that night makes me chuckle, but Jules is wiping away actual tears from laughing so hard. My story is funny. Not as funny as she is laughing at it, but I don't care. Her happiness is all I crave. I will share all my friends' stupid stories and my own.

Right now, she's laughing about that time a bunch of us were on a pub crawl and just happened to walk by a Tae Kwon Do studio with the door open. My friend thought it would be a smart idea to run into the studio screaming.

"Your turn. Best drunk story."

She takes another breath to calm down, while also looking like she's thinking, trying to remember a good story. "Gosh, I am pathetic. I don't really have one. I didn't go away to school. It was close enough that I stayed living at home and commuted."

"What about nights out with friends?"

She worries her bottom lip, looking down and to the side a bit like she's embarrassed.

*Shit.* I want the carefree laughter back.

"Yeah, sorry. I don't have any," she says.

Just then her Mrs. Pacman kills me. Again. "You have to be kidding me." I grunt in frustration. "Stupid game."

"Are you mad at the game or over the fact that I'm beating you?" She looks around the place, then smiles wickedly at me. "Gosh, I've beaten you in almost every game we've played."

I've noticed both last night and tonight that when she seems unsure, she plays with the beads on the string around her wrist. I've also noticed, as the evening has gone on, that she's touched it less and less. It makes me feel like puffing out my chest. It's a stupid reaction, but nonetheless true.

"You're taking a bit too much joy in my misery."

"Now, Hunter, have I wounded your pride? Come on. You can handle a little beat-down."

We've played 75 percent of the games here, and she's killing me. She's good. But to be honest, I think part of me is letting her win because when she does, I'm rewarded. When she wins, she does an enticing victory shimmy dance. I never knew I was an ass man until I saw hers, but damn it I am. And hers is perfect.

When she turns in her latest dance, I step in. As she comes back around to face me, her breath hitches. Her breast grazes my chest. We're so close. I want to pull her to me and devour her mouth. I want to claim her as mine. But the deer-in-head-lights look she's giving me makes me back up to give her space. The last thing I want is to push her too far.

"Tonight has been amazing," she says. "Thank you, Hunter."

"Thank you. It's been a blast."

"What made you think of this?" She looks around us again. "Is this normal for you or..."

"Not normal. Honestly?" I take a moment to look in her eyes. They are deep blue and swallowing me. "You're hard for me to read. I'm constantly torn that you're feeling the same things I am—this connection we have—to feeling like you're just doing this because you're a woman of your word. So, I thought maybe if we were busy having fun, I'd have a better chance of getting to know you. And maybe convince you that me knowing things about you wouldn't be such a bad thing."

"Ah, you were distracting me." She smiles at me, and it is full force and consuming me.

"No, you distract me. I needed something else to focus on to ignore my nerves."

"You don't come across as someone who gets nervous often.

I find it hard to believe I make you nervous. You walked into Portland Social last night and commanded the room."

"You noticed when I walked in?" I can't help my smile.

She looks down at the game, avoiding my eyes. "You're hard not to notice, Hunter."

I don't think she meant to say that out loud for how softly she spoke it. "I don't get nervous easily, Jules. That's what's so distracting about you."

"Your honesty is—"

"Refreshing?" I smile.

She laughs. Again, it covers me, and it's a sound I want to keep hearing. "No. Jarring. I'm not used to adults having so much candor. Kids, yes—they can be brutal in their honesty. But I don't think I'm prepared for you." She quickly glances at my lips. "Again, thank you for tonight."

"It doesn't have to be over. We have more games we could play. Or we could go grab a drink or dessert somewhere. Anything," I offer. Actually, I'm pretty much begging. The thought of this night already ending is torture.

She smiles, looking up at me like she might agree, but then a shadow comes over her eyes. "Ugh, I'm still so full from all the appetizers we had. Seriously. Tonight has been...unexpected."

*Unexpected. Is that positive?* Before I can ask, she takes another step back from me and shakes her head as a blush overtakes her face and chest. I love knowing she's affected as much as I am.

I place my hand on her hip to stop her retreat. "God, you are gorgeous, and funny, and sexy as hell."

She laughs. "Do you ever filter yourself?"

"What's the point? And no, especially not when there's a beautiful soul right in front of me and I can see the walls she's putting between us. Don't, Jules. Please, give me a chance?"

I can't help it. It's like something or someone else takes over my body, and before I can stop myself, I've sliced myself open and laid it all out for her.

She looks scared, and I worry I've messed everything up before ever legitimately getting a shot. But then she surprises me.

She licks her lips, steps toward me, places her left hand behind my neck, and pulls me down. It isn't much of a pull because I willingly go to her. She tastes even sweeter than I thought she would as our mouths crash together. My tongue runs across her bottom lip, begging for entrance. She opens right away, and I own her mouth. My right hand goes under her cardigan to her waist. My thumb meets skin below her tank top, my hand moves to her lower back, and I bring her closer to me.

Even though she's won almost every game tonight, I'm the big winner. And then I feel like a king when I hear it, her small moans, and they only spur me on.

7

JULES

*M*oaning. I am moaning. Lord, I'm the one who started this. I had successfully created space between us, but then his damn words. I have never—*ever*—been with someone so transparent, and I just wanted to live in that for a flash. And yeah, the moan happened because Hunter can kiss. He feels too incredible. Damn, why does his kiss have to feel so promising? *Shit. What am I doing?*

*Get your shit together, Jules. He is trouble, remember?*

My hand presses into Hunter's chest, ultimately breaking our kiss. We're both breathing fast and deep. That was incredible. But I can't do this. He's been clear he wants more. I can't give more. *What am I thinking?*

"If you aren't ready to go, I can call for a ride." *Ugh, that even sounds stupid to me.*

The look on his face tells me he feels the same. "A ride? What?"

"I'm tired, so I just want to head back home. Thanks so much. I really—" I try to brush him off, but Hunter will have none of that. *Shit.* I have awoken the beast, and he's in full alpha mode.

"Go? Tired?" He sounds irritated. I can see him thinking, like he's trying to figure me out. He takes a shaky breath before continuing. "What's going on, beautiful? We've had an amazing night. And that kiss...that kiss was insane, and I know you felt it too." He puts his forehead against mine. "So, why do I feel like you're speeding away?" His left hand moves from the back of my head to the side of my neck. His thumb brushes my lip.

My eyes close and my mouth opens just a fraction. Why is my body so responsive to him? Why does everything feel so superior coming from him? I try to shield my eyes from him, looking off to the side as I step back, breaking our connection.

"Me? No. No. You're right, I had a decidedly nice time. Thank you. But it was just a date, Hunter. And now the date is over. Maybe you aren't told *no* often, but this is me telling you the pleasant night is now over."

"Did I do something?"

*Did he do something?* That's a loaded question.

He kissed me. Well, technically I kissed him first, but losing myself is not something I'm used to. Let alone from a simple kiss. But that kiss was far from simple. Add in the way his hands felt on me, the possessive way he held me; it was all too much. It was too pleasing. Just the way he's looking at me right now with his hazel eyes so dark...

But I can only do simple. I can't do this, with all the feelings it stirs in me. It hurts too much. And Hunter is not simple. I allow myself one last perusal of his frame. Then I turn and start heading to grab my jacket and purse.

"You did nothing wrong, Hunter," I say over my shoulder. "I'm a woman of my word. I lost a bet. I paid my debt. Well, technically you paid, but I came." His eyebrow goes up, and it flusters me. "God, you know what I mean. I accompanied you. And now I'm ready to go back home." At this point I'm facing him but walking backward, toward the exit.

Hunter just stands there for a moment, looking at my face. Studying me. "Who was he?"

That stops my retreat. "Pardon?" I can't tell if he's trying to confuse me so I forget I want to leave, but that's not happening.

"The idiot who hurt you? You are this phenomenal, beautiful, strong, and brave person. But now…now you're acting scared. If you're being honest and I did nothing wrong, then some asshole in your past did, and I'm paying for it. It's probably why you don't date now."

My breath leaves my lungs. I'd love to say what I want to say. I'm not that brave. I am so far from brave I'm at the other end of the spectrum. I can't open myself up and bleed in front of a practical stranger. I can't. I can't even do that with Gretchen, and she probably knows me best. Talking lets others in. And once someone is in, they have the power to hurt me. I can't go through that again. I won't.

"You are that full of yourself? I can't possibly want to end the date? Do I have to be damaged by some bad boy?" I'm reacting now. But no one likes to be psychoanalyzed on a date, let alone a first date. "Sorry to disappoint you, Hunter. There is no idiot. Well, in my past that is. The guy standing before me now is quickly falling into the idiot category, though."

That seems to sink into him. He doesn't even try to fight my words. He looks deep into my eyes, and I will myself not to back down. He gives me a quick nod and walks over to the bar, I assume to settle up.

A few moments later, he walks back over to the front door. He holds it open and motions for me to head out. I shoot a look over to the bartender, who looks like she wishes she had a bowl of popcorn to enjoy with the show we've been giving her. I pick up my jacket and purse and head out the open door.

We walk in silence to his truck. The silence continues the short drive to my place. The only motion is the drumming of his fingers on his right thigh. It produces no noise, though. The silence now falls into the awkward category, and I know I have to say something. I have to put the final nail in this coffin.

"Thank you again, Hunter. I had an enjoyable night. I hope you find whatever you're looking for. And who knows, maybe we'll run into each other again at Portland Social."

He lets out a quick laugh and just shakes his head. *Okay. This is worse than awkward.* He barely has the truck stopped when I all but fly out of it. I hear him say something, but between how quickly I'm putting distance between us and the rushing of blood in my ears, I can't hear him.

8

HUNTER

*W*hat the fuck? Seriously. What the actual fuck just happened? The night was good. It was amazing. And that kiss. That kiss was going somewhere. And then, she flipped the switch and ran. Literally. She ran from my truck. I'm too amped up right now to go to my empty home.

As I walk into Portland Social, I'm relieved to see Chase behind the bar. He's down on the left talking with a guy, so I head their way.

"Hunter?" he says quizzically. "Oh, no. What did you do wrong?"

"What is that supposed to mean?"

"Wasn't tonight the date-bet night? It's ten, dude, and you're standing in front of me instead of a beautiful blonde. So, what did you do wrong?"

Before I answer, I glance to my side—to the guy on my left that Chase was talking to.

"Hunter, Aiden. Aiden, Hunter," Chase introduces us.

We shake hands. The guy is sitting down with a baseball hat pulled low. Even sitting, I can tell he's tall.

I think he's the same guy who was here last night sitting in the same spot all alone. "Have we met before? You look familiar."

Chase does a quick headshake, silently telling me to drop it before Aiden speaks.

"Nah, I don't think so, man."

"So, Hunter," Chase says, "you were about to tell us what you did to already mess up your chance with the beautiful and tantalizing Jules."

"Nothing. I don't think I did anything wrong. That's what has me so baffled. We were having an amazing time. We were laughing, and everything was going great. Then she just morphed into this cold robot. We were kissing and I had her pressed up against me, and in an instant, she was running from me. Literally *running* away from me. It was weird."

"Doesn't sound weird to me," Aiden says. "It sounds like she got scared. You might not have intentionally done anything to scare her, but she got spooked." Aiden spills his wisdom without ever lifting his gaze from his beer.

"What the hell? I thought the bartender was the one that was supposed to wax poetic. Are you listening to this, Chase? It seems you have a bar Yoda," I say, slapping Aiden on the back.

"Well, what are you going to do about it—about Jules, that is?" Chase grabs a bar rag and wipes up the area in front of me before placing an old-fashioned in front of me that I didn't order.

I look up to Chase as he talks, and I sigh out of frustration. "I don't have a damn clue. I feel like she's worth it, though. She's worth trying for, I can tell you that. But how do you win someone over who claims they don't want anything to do with you? We had a marvelous night. I don't think I've ever laughed that much on a date. There were no awkward silences or struggles for conversation. It was perfect."

"Except for the fleeing. When she ran away from you. That

seems like a big negative against you," Chase offers up with a grin the size of Texas.

Aiden laughs at Chase's comment and then he says, "Make the offer too tempting." He isn't even looking at me, choosing instead to stare at his half-empty beer.

"What do you mean?" I ask him.

Aiden looks up, but at the TV, not me. "You like this girl, right?"

I look over to Chase and shake my head at Aiden's obviously stupid question. *Why else would I be acting like this?* "Yeah. I like her."

"So, if you like her so much, figure out what she won't say no to as an ingrained response. Make her think about it. Make her think about *you*. Figure out what she cares about, and make it too tempting to say no." Aiden still doesn't look at me.

Chase and I both look to Aiden and laugh at his wisdom once again.

I slap my hand on his shoulder. Seriously, this guy is brilliant. "His next drink is on me."

*Make the offer too tempting.* Sounds simple.

I SPEND another hour hanging at the bar, talking with Chase and Aiden about the MLB playoffs and the start of basketball. I call my car service to pick me up. I'll get my truck tomorrow. By the time I make it back home, I'm less tense.

As I lie in my king-size bed, replaying the date in my mind, I try picking everything apart to figure out what went wrong. I don't think I was too pushy. She seemed like she felt the same things I was feeling, and I guess that scared her and made her run. I am not being overly confident; the night was good. There isn't anything I can look at and say, *"Oh, that was when I did it."*

I was honest with her, though. And that ruffled her a bit.

Aiden was right; she got spooked.

Now I need to figure out how to tempt her. What's something she won't shoot down right away? I just need to figure out how to get more time with her.

9

## JULES

$\mathcal{I}$ try to enter our apartment as quietly as possible so as not to disturb Gretchen. However, she's sitting in the main room.

"Home already? I thought Hunter had more game than that. It must have been bad."

"What? No. It was fine."

"Fine? That is female code for *it sucked*."

I want to lie to her. I want to say that it sucked. But whereas before, with Hunter, I couldn't seem to tell the truth, with Gretchen, I can't lie.

"It was astonishing. The evening was perfect." As soon as the words are out, my air whooshes and I place my head in my hands. *I will not cry. I will not cry.* I repeat it to myself like a mantra.

"Um, hon, *perfect* doesn't usually look like this," she says, waving her hands around. "Jules, it's me. Talk to me. I'm right here." She squeezes my hand.

I look back up at her. "It was unbelievable. Have you heard of Ground Control?"

"The arcade place for adults?"

"Yes, that's the place. Well, he knows the owners, and I guess they closed for a bit because of a big remodel. Anyway, they were trying recipes and such today, so Hunter asked if some staff could stay on so we could use the place. Gretch, we just had fun and spent time together. And the fact that the entire time we were busy doing something, it made the conversation so easy."

"Okay. Well, this all sounds great. So, again, why do you look the way you do?"

"I can't, Gretchen. I can just tell. He's a guy that would bulldoze my walls."

"I love you, girl. I'm here for you." She pauses. "But we've lived together for a bit, and I don't know much more about you than I did when we first moved in together. I appreciate how you're here for me. But you definitely keep people a few car lengths away from you. I think you need someone who's able to get through those walls of yours. Hell, one night with him and you've already made progress. You just admitted you have walls up. That's more than you've admitted in the time we've known each other."

She means well, but I can't help the anger brewing in me. I'm mad at myself. I'm mad that I let Hunter affect me the way he has. I'm also upset I'm not in his bed with him right now. But, mostly, I'm upset with how I treated him. He probably hates me now. That's a good thing, right? I want him to be happy.

My mind flashes to the thought of him being happy with someone else—maybe the hostess at Ground Control; she kept looking at him dreamily—and my stomach sours.

I bring myself back into the present and focus on what Gretchen said. My anger is misplaced, but I don't seem to care tonight. She's here, so it's easier to direct it at her than at myself.

"Oh, and you're such an open book? Please. I think the

reason you like me so much is that I don't push. I know there's more to you and Chase. If we're breaking down walls, let's start with that one."

I'm seething. But she's right. I decided after losing Mitch and Matt that I wouldn't let anyone that close again. If they're not close, then it won't hurt as much when they leave.

"Touchy much?" She recoils and rolls her eyes. I expect her to lash back at me. Instead, she takes a breath, then looks at me. "Yeah, you're right. There is more when it comes to me and Chase, but that's a conversation all on its own, okay? Right now, Ms. Deflector, we're talking about you."

Everything in me seems ready to boil over. "My brother died years ago," I blurt. I can't look at her. My scrutiny is fixed on the beads of my bracelet. If I meet her eyes, my composure will be gone. And right now, control of myself is all I have.

"What? I mean, you've talked about Mitch but not a ton. I just figured there was some family drama there, and I didn't want to pry. Oh, Jules." She hugs me and I stiffen, but the contact still feels nice. "Okay, I feel like this conversation needs wine. Hold on."

Gretchen rises from the couch and goes to open a bottle from a winery we visited a couple of months ago. A group of staff from school went. I offered to be the designated driver. It was quite an experience for me. Teachers gone wild.

She comes back to the couch—bottle tucked under her arm, two glasses in her hands—and she sits. "Okay, take this glass. Now talk," Gretchen says, before taking a sip of her wine.

"I think I mentioned that we were close in age," I say, and Gretchen nods. "We were just over a year apart. My brother was spectacular, my best friend. I miss him every day. Every damn day." A tear escapes my restraint. As it falls and lands in my wineglass, I watch as it makes a ripple. I reach over and place my glass on our coffee table.

After a moment, I look at Gretchen. I give her a small smile, trying to let her in a bit. "He played football at our high school. He was a running back. I remember as young as five being at his flag football games. He liked the study of the game. The plays, the possibilities. The way one had to push themselves, always."

"Mitch sounds incredible, just like his sister," Gretchen whispers.

I smile as more tears fall. It feels so cathartic to be talking about him, but it breaks me at the same time. "He was wonderful."

"May I ask what happened?"

"I was seventeen, he was eighteen. He was at football practice. He usually drove a friend home from practice, but that night he was driving straight to our house. He was going around a turn, and another car was coming at him, in Mitch's lane. He was hit head-on."

"Oh my gosh." Her right hand covers her mouth as her eyes fill with tears. "How awful for you and your parents. I can't imagine." She puts her hand on my knee and squeezes; it reminds me of something my mom would do.

"It turns out the other driver was drunk. He'd lost his license and had his car impounded just weeks earlier. But he borrowed his neighbor's car that night. That asshole is fine. He's serving time now, but one day he'll be out and about like nothing ever happened. My brother fought, but his injuries were too bad. He passed early the next morning. Mitch shouldn't have been there at that moment, but he changed his routine to come right home from practice. Life just sucks sometimes." I try to smile at her to lighten the mood, but my smile isn't genuine.

I roll my head around slowly, pausing and trying to crack my neck. I look down and see this one small stain, a teardrop of red wine Gretchen must have spilled. I just look at it, trying to control my heart rate, thinking about that awful time in my life. My memories crash over me, like the dam broke that was holding them back.

I take a deep, stuttered breath, snapping myself out of my past. I can't tell her about Matt. Not right now. It would be too much. Maybe another day.

"I am so sorry you had to lose him that way. I don't want to dismiss all those feelings. But I have to ask, hon." She bites the side of her lip, almost holding herself back. "What does losing your brother have to do with pushing Hunter away?"

"I'm not ready."

"Ready for what?" Gretchen asks quietly.

"I'm not ready to let someone get close."

"What do you mean?"

"People date because they want to get to know each other, to become closer. They continue dating because they feel a need inside to continue finding things out about the other person. The end goal is usually to see how compatible they are together. I can't do that—any of it. I don't want to let someone in, because I won't survive if they leave when they stop wanting to discover what makes me *me*. Or worse, if they are taken from me." It feels like such a weight on my chest, constantly worrying and trying to control it all.

"So, your answer is to never let yourself be happy?"

"I am happy," I argue.

Gretchen looks at me, and a crease forms where her eyebrows draw together. "Are you really happy? I mean, truly, at the end of the day, do you feel inside that you are happy?"

"I don't know if I have been since the accident," I admit.

"How long has it been?"

"There's no timeline on grief. I'm so tired of people telling me how to process. How I should move on. How I need to find someone to be close to."

"I realize there's no timeline. Do you think you'd want to get close to Hunter?"

"I see something in his eyes that almost mirrors me. I don't know what it is. But I can just tell, with him, all my keep-it-simple strategies won't work. I can feel it. So, I pushed him away. Damn, I was a bitch." I rest my fingers on my lips, lightly brushing them.

"Did you kiss him?"

"What? Why would you ask that?"

"Because you keep skimming your lips, and you're blushing. Something tells me you did, and it was epic."

I groan. "Gretch, it was incredible." I lean back and cover my face with a pillow.

"So, the hot man who obviously wants you is a nonstarter because you want him back, and...you just aren't ready? Are you sure?"

"Yeah. I have to be."

"Well, cheers to you. You have way more self-control than I do." Gretchen reaches over and refills her wineglass.

One glass in, and I feel like I can push her a bit more. Plus, I desperately want to get the subject off me. "So, back to there being more to the Chase story. Care to share? You know, since we're sharing."

She groans, and I don't think I'm going to get anything out of her until she speaks. "Let's just say Chase Carmichael was someone special to me. He probably always will be. Some shit went down, and what I had *hoped* would happen between us went away. Any chance of it. So now, I honestly just want to be friends with him. We actually went to high school together too, so he's someone I've known for over a decade. I don't know if he even wants to be friends, though. So, I'm just trying. That's all."

My roommate is striking. Her smooth amber hair is a beacon for attention. However, she always shies away from it. She harps about my love life, but I've never seen her serious about anyone, either.

As I look at her now, I see the same veil of sadness I see

when she thinks no one is paying attention. "What are you thinking?"

"Honestly?" She stops swirling her wine, lifts her eyes to me, and offers a small smile. "Of all people, I don't understand why it took you so long to tell *me* about him. Your brother. Didn't you think I'd understand?"

I look up at the ceiling, trying to find the words to explain. I get what she's saying.

She hasn't lost anyone like I have, but her mom left her when she was little—just took off. A loss is a loss.

"It's never been about someone else understanding. I think for a long time it was about not wanting to share. Like if I told others, I'd be giving away pieces of him. I wanted to keep all of him to myself. I guess I'm selfish." I shrug and smile at her, hoping maybe she'll get where I'm coming from.

"You are far from selfish. But I do think you close yourself off. If you don't want Hunter, fine. But try to open yourself enough that there's at least a possibility for someone. Right now, I don't think anyone could get through without a machete."

We laugh and stay up way too late. The next morning, I think again of what she said.

A machete might not get through my walls; they're rock and supported with steel beams. One would need a sledgehammer to break apart the mortar between the stones. But before anything, I'd have to let the sledgehammer near me. And that can't happen as long as I keep an observant eye on what might be coming.

# HUNTER

*Thurs. Oct 29th*
**Me**: Sorry it's taken days for me to text, but things with work have been crazy. I know our date last weekend didn't end the best, but up until the end, I felt like we had a great time. I just wanted to tell you you're on my mind. You said Halloween is crazy in your classroom, so I'm sending luck from China.

*WED. Nov 4th*
**Me**: I saw voters passed the school bond for your district. That's great. I hope the funds flow to your school and benefit your kids. I hope you are well.

*SUN. Nov 15th*
**Me**: At Portland Social and just beat Chase at darts, and it made me think of you. Tell me to stop texting and I will. I don't want to bother you. Otherwise, I'll keep reaching out hoping you'll respond. I hope you are well.

. . .

*Thurs. Nov 26th*
   **Me**: Happy Thanksgiving, Jules.

SITTING at my desk at work, I'm aware I should go over the file my assistant gave me. Instead, I'm staring at my phone, at my unanswered texts. It's been almost a week since I sent my last text. I should stop texting her. Chase said I'm skating the line of being creepy. I told her to tell me to stop, though. If she wanted me to. She hasn't responded to anything. It's been just over a month now, and I still can't stop thinking about her. The frequency has dwindled, but every now and then, the thought of her floats through my mind.

Before I can think better of it, I dial the number I got from Chase.

"Hello?"

"So, I want to run an idea by you," I say into the phone as I pace in my office.

"Most people say, '*Hello, this is so and so.*' How about we start there?"

I laugh nervously. "Hello, Gretchen. This is Hunter. I have an idea I want to run by you."

"I'm listening."

Aiden said I'd have to tempt Jules, but I didn't think it would take me this long to come up with something. When I was talking with my assistant this week about her holiday, she mentioned her daughter—who's a teacher. She said it was so nice to see her relax and get away from things. It clicked then.

I clear my throat before laying out my proposal. "I have a house up in Government Camp on Mt. Hood. Chase and I are heading up there this weekend, and we thought it'd be cool if you and Jules came too. No strings, just a relaxing weekend away from the city."

The line is quiet for so long I pull my phone away from my

ear to make sure it's still connected.

"By *no strings,* you mean…"

"Just that. We're all going as friends. Or I guess, potential friends. The place is enormous. I had it built for retreats for work and such, so there are plenty of rooms and beds. Honest. We just want a weekend away and thought it'd be fun to hang with you girls. And that maybe you guys could use a weekend away too."

Gretchen blows out a deep sigh. "Why are you calling me instead of her?"

"Fair question. I figured I had a better chance of you answering than her. She's either ignoring me or has me blocked." She makes an *mm-hmm* sound on the other end in agreement. I'm not sure to which. "Plus, maybe you could phrase it better than me and have a better chance of convincing her."

"That is honest and accurate. And Chase knows you're inviting me too?"

I pause for a second, thrown by her question. "Yes, he knows. Why?" When I brought up the idea to Chase, he told me I was insane. But he never said he had a problem with Gretchen coming.

"Just checking. Give me a bit and I'll text you and let you know."

"Great. This is my cell, so just text this number. Thanks, Gretchen."

Now all there is to do is sit back and hope this works. I just need more time with Jules. Maybe then we can see if there really is something there. Or, I can squash it and put all of this in the past.

But…I hope Gretchen can convince her.

# 11

## JULES

$\mathcal{T}$he weeks leading up to Thanksgiving break were crazy with work. I had planned on going home for Thanksgiving, but my parents informed me they'd booked a last-minute cruise. Though I knew they just wanted to get out of town around this time of year. I couldn't blame them. Gretchen was incredible and brought me home to her grandma's. As we drove back to Portland from Olympia at the end of Thanksgiving weekend, Gretchen proposed another getaway.

"So, a friend offered their place next weekend if you want to head up to Government Camp. We have that Friday off from the kids to finish up report cards, but I thought maybe if we pushed ourselves, we could be done by midday and head up to the mountain. They got an early snowfall up there, so things are opening early."

"Oh, that sounds great. I'd love to see some snow. I'm not much of a skier, but I'm sure there are other things to do up there."

"Great. I'll text my friend and set it all up."

BY THE TIME Friday comes around, I am beyond ready for a weekend away. I woke up at 4:30 in the morning to finish the kids' report cards so we could get out of town at a decent time and still arrive with daylight left. I finish grades and then work on my donor project I'm setting up for my classroom. I need Chromebooks for my whole class, and our district doesn't have the money to supply them. Other teachers have had success, so I hope I will too.

I understand I *just* went out of town, but a holiday weekend with Gretchen and her grandma (while great) is much different than a quiet weekend away with a friend.

I haven't been out with anyone since my date with Hunter. He called and texted a few times but has since stopped. I was nervous the other week when Gretchen and I stopped into Portland Social. I don't know if I was more worried he would be there or that he wouldn't be. Turns out, I was a bit disappointed when he wasn't there. Gretchen picked up on it and tried to get me to call him. But it's for the best if we stay away from each other.

As I pack the last of my stuff, my phone rings. I look and see that it's Eric. This is his second call this month. The last one I let go to voicemail. I steady myself before answering. I feel guilty that I'm answering now only because we're leaving soon, so I'll have an excuse to get off the phone quickly.

"Hello!" I try to sound cheery.

"Well, that is one heck of a hello."

Apparently, I oversold my joy in talking with him. Eric isn't a bad guy. He just tries too hard. Even after all this time, it's hard to be around him. He looks too much like Matt. The same blond wavy hair. The same color eyes. However, I don't get lost in his.

Two months after the funeral, I had a weak moment where we kissed. I'd gotten momentarily swept away in his blue eyes, so similar to his brother's. The instant our lips touched, I regretted it. I was looking for Matt. It wasn't fair to Eric, and it wasn't fair to me. After he asked me for a chance, he said he's always wanted me. I told him I saw him as just a friend, and that the kiss had confirmed it for me. I blame myself for it, but since then, things have shifted with us.

He's never asked for another chance, but I know he still wants one. He's so involved in my parents' lives and is always checking on me. It should be sweet, but it just makes me feel guilty. I've never talked to him about my relationship with his brother.

Shaking my head and crawling out of the past, I hear Eric chuckle on the other end.

"Sorry, Eric. I'm running around like crazy trying to get out of town."

"Ah, yes. I ran into your dad just a few minutes ago at Green Plow when I stopped in to refuel on some coffee. He said they had a great time on their cruise and that you were going up to Mt. Hood. I see, even years later, they still leave town around this time of year. You, though...you just left us all, so I still blame you. When are you coming back to us, Jules?"

"Back?"

"Well, I'd like you back forever. But at least a visit would be nice. I'm sure it would mean a lot to your parents."

It feels like every conversation is the same. He always brings up how much I'm hurting my parents by being away. It was hard on my mom at first. But they seem better with it now. I think.

"Well, I didn't know you were calling to guilt trip me, Eric. I shouldn't have answered," I bite out.

That was rude. I don't want to be rude to him. But Eric always acts like he's holding out for me. Like eventually, I'll come around. And I won't. I've told him that, but it doesn't seem to matter.

He blows out a breath. "I'm sorry, you're right. I didn't call you to give you a guilt trip, I swear. I just miss you, Jules."

"I'll be home for Christmas. It's just a few weeks away. But this really isn't a good time. As I said, I'm heading out in a bit for the weekend."

Eric chokes. "Damn it, I got coffee all over my uniform. That's right. Weekend, huh? Who are you going with?" he asks, the jealousy in his voice coming through crystal clear.

"Gretchen."

"That's your roommate, right? That sounds fine."

*Fine? Ugh.* I should have lied and told him I was going away with a guy. Maybe he'd move on. But it would get back to my parents, and no reprieve from Eric's attention is worth that interrogation.

"Babe, you ready? Let's hit the road before we have to deal with traffic," Gretchen yells from her room.

Moving my phone away from my mouth, I yell back, "Packed and ready, Gretch." I bring the phone back, ready to get off this call. "Hey, Eric, I really have to go. I'll see you when I'm home for Christmas, okay?"

"Looking forward to it. Bye, Jules."

I walk out of my room and stop in front of Gretchen's open door. I place my duffle bag on the ground.

"Is that small bag all you're bringing?" Gretchen asks as she eyes it.

"Yeah, it's just us so I don't need anything to impress. I have my sweats, a swimsuit in case there's a hot tub, and that's about it."

"Huh, okay. Well, if we're feeling up to it, we might go out one night. Just pack a few extra things so you have options." She smiles at me innocently. "I'm so excited. I think this weekend is going to be just what you need."

"Just what I need? Nope. It's what *we* need."

"Yes. What we need." She bites her lip.

We bring our bags down to Gretchen's car and toss them in her trunk.

Getting out of Portland doesn't take much time, and before I know it, we're on Highway 26 leading us to Mt. Hood. Usually, when I'm a passenger in a car for longer than a quick commute, I fall asleep. I've been told I make a horrible road companion. Today is no different as I wake when Gretchen pulls off the highway about an hour and a half after we left.

"That was fast. Are we already here?"

"Ha. Of course it's fast when you take your time-machine nap and sleep the whole trip."

"Sorry. Everything looks so beautiful covered in snow. I can't believe I haven't come up here yet. How do you know the person whose place we're staying at?"

"Uh...shh, I need to focus on finding it, and the road is a bit icy." She pulls off the main road and down a street of beautiful cabins and homes.

We pull up to three stories of amazingness. There's a three-car garage on the left, a beautiful, curved door in the middle with two stories of windows above it, and more house on the right. There are one, two...*five* decks from what I can see from the front. As the shock wears off that this is where I get to spend the next couple of days, it registers how nervous Gretchen is acting.

"What's going on? This place looks awesome. Why do you look nervous? I can't believe you have friends that own a place like this."

"What do you mean?" she asks, chewing on her upper lip. It's a sure sign something is definitely up. "Jules, just remember how much I love you, okay? And that I just want you to be happy."

"Gretchen, what's going on?" I search her face and look around at the house and area again. Then, a little voice inside speaks to me. *This house is insane. Who could afford a place like this?* "Gretchen...whose house is this?"

She laughs nervously, refusing to look me in the eye. "Well, I don't know many people that could afford a place like this.

They'd have to be a billionaire." She speaks so quickly and gives me the guiltiest grin.

"Mother—"

Before I can finish, movement on my right grabs my attention. I shift in my seat, now facing forward, and standing before me is Chase. Next to him, looking so delectable, is Hunter. Both of them are smiling at us. Before I can continue yelling at her, Gretchen hops out of the car as fast as she can.

"Gretchen, get back in the car!" I whisper-yell, but it's too late.

She totally set me up. This is not good. I'm going to kill her.

I'm sitting in front of one of the most marvelous homes I've ever seen, with three people looking at me expectantly. I have my eyes closed now, trying to calm myself down like I teach my kinders to do. Deep breath in, and then slowly exhale. It isn't working.

With my eyes closed, I don't see someone come over. Yet, I feel the cold air rush in as my door opens. I hear the voice. His delicious, husky voice. I smell him. I take another deep breath, but not to calm myself. I give myself a few seconds to enjoy his scent, and it makes me shift a bit in my seat. It's been more than a month since our date.

"I don't understand what you're doing, beautiful. Do you think if you keep your eyes shut, we can't see you?" Then the bastard laughs.

"Did you know?" I'm so angry. I feel ambushed.

"Know what?" He sounds genuinely confused.

"That I'd be here?" I finally open my eyes and look at him, and my heart beats even faster. Weeks later, and he still affects me.

"Uh, yeah." His brows pull together. He searches my face. "This is my house, Jules. I invited you guys to come up." I can tell he sees the surprise mixed with the anger on my face, as well as my tense shoulders. "Wait, did you not know I'd be here?" he asks.

I look at him. He's crouched down by my open passenger door. I see his confusion clear as day, and my temper toward him dissipates. "No. No, Hunter, I had no idea." I glance over to a guilty-looking Gretchen before looking back at him. "Someone told me it was a girls' weekend."

Both our eyes shoot to Gretchen, and she braves speaking to me.

"To be fair, I asked if you wanted to get away and said I had a place. You assumed it would just be us, and I didn't dissuade that thinking. That's all I'm guilty of. Honestly, it's just poor communication." She smiles sweetly, like she's the most innocent being.

Hunter looks stuck. He tries to say something, but nothing comes out. Finally, he clears his throat. "Listen. I'm sincerely sorry. I thought you knew. Clearly you didn't, but I'd like you to stay, Jules. For both of you to stay. What do you say?"

"You're too much," I mutter, hopefully quiet enough that Hunter doesn't hear, but by the smile taking over his face, he did. *I am so screwed.*

"Jules, I want you to know I wouldn't trick you into hanging out with me."

"You mean like making a bet and making me go out with you." *Okay, that was bitchy.* I understand this is all on Gretchen. But I'm still irritated at being tricked, regardless of who was behind it.

"Shit." He runs his hands through his hair and stands up, starting to pace. "I don't get a lot of time off. I thought it would be nice to come up here, and when I talked to Chase about it, we thought of you guys right away. I know you don't want to date me. I promise I heard you that night. And if I didn't, trust me, I got the hint from you ghosting me. But we still had a lot of fun and got along easily. I know now that this was a stupid idea, though."

He stops pacing and looks down at me. "If you want to go, I understand. But I truly would love for you to stay and have a fun weekend up here. That's all. I promise. I lost control of this situation fast. But that seems to be the norm when I'm around you. There. That's my sales pitch. Take it for what you want."

I look from him to the house again and back to him. "I want to see the house first, then I'll decide."

Finally, a smile returns to his face. "Ouch. Am I not enough for you?" He puts his hand on his chest, feigning injury. Then, he laughs as he moves aside, giving me room to get out of the car. He reaches his hand out to help me.

I stare at his hand and remember the way it felt on my body. My cheeks heat at the memory. What is wrong with me when I'm around this guy? I've dated. I've slept with guys. But this one. This one throws me for a loop without even really doing anything.

I exit Gretchen's car without taking Hunter's outstretched hand. The less contact, the better.

"Let me grab your bags for you, and I'll show you around. You and Gretchen." He reaches for the bags in the trunk.

"That isn't necessary. We don't know if we'll be staying yet."

"Right." He looks at the bag like he wants to say more but is holding himself back.

"What?"

"I was just thinking, how about we bring in your bags and just leave them in the foyer? That way your stuff is in there if you decide to stay." He steps in closer to me. "Because I'm confident you're going to want to."

My breathing quickens, and I'm sure he notices I'm affected by how close he is to me. We both just stand there, looking at each other.

He clears his throat and grabs our three bags. "Is this all? For both of you?" he questions.

"Those two are Gretchen's. Just the camo bag is mine."

"Well, let's head in. Right this way, girls. Make sure you watch your step. We had some storms this week and I'd hate for either of you to fall on any slick spots."

I can feel him watching me as I look around, taking it all in.

It won't be light out for much longer; winter nights in Oregon get dark early. I walk behind Hunter as he opens the massive wood door and leads us into his warm house. It's the only way I can describe it.

The foyer is profoundly masculine. The floors are dark slate, the walls are river rock, and the ceiling has wood slats with beams. The foyer is also bigger than normal. There's a bench in front of two massive closets. Three other chairs, and a large, mirrored piece of furniture with drawers.

Hunter must see me inspecting it, because he says, "I have no idea what that's called, but I like it. The decorator sent me different options, and it was the one that jumped out at me. I wanted an area that wouldn't feel crowded while people arrived or got ready to head out."

"You accomplished it," I tell him. "This is beautiful."

"Thank you. I love it. But I also love seeing others' faces as they see it for the first time. I put a lot of time into picking everything out."

"You built this? Well, I mean, you had this place built?" I don't know why I'm shocked.

"Yes. It took longer than it should have, but I'm so happy with how it turned out." He looks around with a satisfied grin on his face.

"I'd definitely say it was worth it," Gretchen chimes in.

I'd nearly forgotten she and Chase were here. I glare at her as I walk past her and further into the house. "It definitely was worth it, I agree. It's awe-inspiring."

"I find the things I work the hardest for are usually the most gratifying," Hunter says.

When I look at him, I see he's staring right at me. My lips part slightly.

Chase clears his throat, and Gretchen laughs.

"I told myself I wouldn't come on strong, that I'd let it build. But damn, I feel like I'm on a timer with you and I have to accomplish as much as I can before it goes off," Hunter confesses.

"Damn you and your honesty." I shake my head.

He leaves our bags in the foyer, and the four of us move through the house. We all walk into the great room. The back wall is all windows, looking out onto the forest. The massive two-story river rock fireplace is against the left wall. There are four different couches.

"My decorator thought it was odd to have different couches. I wanted my guests to feel like they had a choice and could be comfortable."

I smile at his candor and the thoughtfulness for his guests. I head toward the leather couch against the back wall.

"That's my favorite," Hunter shares.

I sit with my one leg tucked under me, angled so I can see out the window. I don't know when I start to pet the faux-fur gray ombré throw that lies over the back, but it entrances me. "I can see why this one is your favorite. You made such a large space so cozy." I find him in the window's reflection and see he's pleased with my comment.

"Hunter, this place is breathtaking," Gretchen says. "Thank you so much for inviting us. We're so happy to be here. Right, Jules?" she adds, prompting me to agree.

I don't answer right away, still petting. "Can we see the room situation before I agree to happily be here?" I close my eyes. Even I can hear the bite in my words. "Sorry, I'm not trying to be a bitch. May I please see what the sleeping arrangements would be?" I look over at Hunter and again, I catch him looking at me. I look away.

"Of course. I'd never want you to be uncomfortable. There are multiple rooms upstairs to choose from. Follow me," he says, and then we head up the massive wood stairs. "I had logs cut in half to make each step. Sorry, I love details. I forget sometimes that others may not. Just tell me to stop if you don't care."

"I love hearing about all the idiosyncrasies." I really do. I love knowing what makes people pick things.

"My room is downstairs. There are two rooms down to the left. Chase is sleeping down that way. There is also an office set up in a room down there. Then two rooms are down on the right, this way. There's a room with a queen—you ladies could share that, or the last room, which is the bunk room. There are four bunk beds built in. I assume you'd want to stay in the same room. But honestly, do whatever you two want."

Gretchen and I look at each other, having a silent conversation. After a bit, I close my eyes and give her a quick nod.

Gretchen speaks for us, then. "This is perfect, Hunter. We'd love to stay, and we'll take the bunk room. It's beautiful."

"Great. I'll run down and get your bags, and you ladies can get settled. I'm happy to have you here. Both of you."

Gretchen looks over at Hunter and gives him a sympathetic smile.

I close the door after Hunter returns with our bags and leaves us to relax for a bit. We tell them we'll be down in about an hour.

"I am still pissed at you," I say to Gretchen.

"Jules, I thought I was doing what was best for you."

"No. What gives you the right to decide what's best for me?"

"Ugh. I meant well, okay? You deserve to have some fun. And maybe, just maybe, have a guy fawn over you. If after this weekend you want absolutely nothing to do with Hunter, I promise I'll stop pushing."

# 90 | QUINN MILLER

"You promise?"

"Promise. But look at this place, hon. It's extraordinary."

She's right. The house is amazing.

*One weekend. It's just one weekend.* I'll have some fun. There's nothing to worry about.

We find Chase and Hunter downstairs about an hour later. I feel a bit more relaxed.

"So, any ideas for tonight?" I ask once we're all situated around the kitchen island.

"Chase, want to tell them?" Hunter prompts.

"Sure, man. So, it might sound a bit lame, but I thought it'd be fun to head over to the ski resort and go cosmic tubing."

Gretchen and I look at each other, visibly confused.

"Cosmic tubing is on one side of the resort; skiing is on the other. They have regular tubing during the day, and at night they have music and lasers. The runs are already groomed and they have a conveyor belt to take you up to the top. It sounds odd, but I promise it'll be fun," Chase offers up, hoping to sway us.

"Oh, and if either of you forgot any winter gear, I have full stock in different sizes in one of the closets in the foyer," Hunter adds. "So, no worries there. When I had this place built, I figured I could use this space not only for work purposes but as a fun getaway spot with friends, too. Some people—clients or otherwise—might fly in and drive up here and they might not pack bulky items, so I just prepared. That's why I have an office set up upstairs just for guests. Because I like to be prepared."

"Well, I think it sounds like a blast. How about some food first, then we can all head over? Gosh, I don't think I've gone tubing since I was a kid." Gretchen looks excited.

"I think it sounds fun, too. How can I help with dinner?" I ask.

"Let me and Chase take care of that. You ladies help yourself to a drink, and we'll eat shortly."

# JULES

"*D*inner is served," Chase greets us as we enter the kitchen.

I'm still a little irritated with how Gretchen handled all of this, but I do feel more tranquil.

*Damn.* Hunter stands in front of us, his short brown hair pushed back and showing off his natural highlights. He has some scruff, and he looks desirable like this. His hazel eyes meet mine, and he smiles. My heartbeat speeds up. *One weekend. It's just one weekend.*

"It smells delicious. What are you two serving?" I try to peek at the dishes on the island.

They made tri-tip, red potatoes, and a salad. I soon discover it's all delicious. It surprises me how easy the conversation is with the four of us. I don't remember the last time I've laughed this hard. I laugh so hard at one point I start crying.

After dinner, we all get ready to go tubing. The guys fill up some flasks to take over with us. *"To keep us warm."*

Now, Hunter joins us in the parking lot after paying for our tubing. "All set."

We walk over to the tubes first, where we each get solo ones.

Then we head over to the conveyor belt that'll take us to the top.

"This is awesome. It's like lazy people's tubing. I always remember hating having to climb up the hills when I was little." I'm smiling so much my cheeks hurt.

Hunter takes out a flask from his coat and offers us all some whiskey. Gretchen takes a sip first. She passes it to Chase who offers it to me. However, I see we're near the top and give a heads-up to Gretchen, who's in front. Hunter puts it back away. We all get in different lanes and race down. I scream and laugh the entire way.

Chase is the first one at the bottom. Gretchen got flipped halfway down, so she's last.

She comes limping over to us, laughing. "Damn, that hurt."

"Then why are you laughing, fool?" I joke.

"Because it was so fun. Let's do it again, but this time, let's use the double tubes."

"Guys against girls?" I suggest.

"We'd win," Hunter replies. "We weigh more, so we'll go faster. It makes sense to do guy/girl." He looks expectantly at me like he's waiting for me to argue.

It's just a tube ride. "Sounds fair."

"Fair, huh? That's a safe response." He doesn't say it rudely. He smiles at me widely like he knows me and what I'm thinking, and it's unnerving.

As we wait in line, Hunter puts his gloved hand on my waist to move me over when a little boy wants to get in line with his dad. I have leggings, ski pants, and a ski coat on, so I shouldn't be able to feel the heat of his hand. It should be impossible. But somehow, I do.

Involuntarily, I lean back a bit and rest against his chest. He leaves his hand on my hip and puts his chin on top of my head. I don't question why I'm not moving. But this feels incredible, and nothing is really even happening.

The employee yells, "Ready, set, *go!*"

The little boy's father goes. Then I notice that the little boy starts to cry.

"Hey now, what's wrong?" I ask, stepping forward and squatting down to talk to him.

"I-I-I don't know how to get in." He tries wiping away his tears, but with his gloves on, he can't. "I don't want to go by myself." With sad puppy eyes, he looks at me with a trembling chin.

I take one glove off and wipe his face. "Oh my goodness. I understand that, but I can help if you'd like."

"No. I don't want to go." He shakes his head.

"Okay. Okay. Is your mommy up here?" I ask, looking around at the other lines of tubers.

"No, I just came with my daddy." *Great. Why would he have gone first?* As if he can read my mind he says, "I told him to go first so he could catch me."

I guess that makes sense. "Well, I'm here with my friend." I point behind me. "This is Hunter. My name is Jules. I have an idea. We have a tube that seats two. You can ride with one of us, and the other can take your tube."

He looks from me to Hunter like he's judging who would be the best partner. "He looks stronger. Can I go with him?"

I smile, pretty confident I'd pick Hunter too. "Sure. You two go, and I'll take yours."

Hunter gives the little boy a high-five and sets him in the front tube, then gives me a wink.

When the tube guy yells, *"Go,"* they take off. I watch with wonder as they descend. I can hear the little boy's screams of glee all the way as they safely make it to the bottom. The little boy's father runs over and grabs his son in a hug before shaking Hunter's hand. And then it's my turn to go. They're off to the side and talking by the time I make it down.

"Jules, this is Nate. He and Troy are having a guys' night."

Nate thanks me for our help with Troy, and then they head off.

Hunter stands to my side, with his arm around me. He turns to me with a huge grin as he looks at me. "You're great with kids. I can see why you went into teaching. You didn't even hesitate to help that little boy. You have an empathetic heart, Jules."

"You do, too. Thanks for just taking off with him and not getting weird about helping." If possible, Hunter is even more attractive in this moment.

"I'm not sure where Gretchen and Chase are. Would you like to try again for our run?" He looks down at me hopefully.

"I'd like that."

We do two more runs before we go looking for Gretchen and Chase. It's odd to be trudging through the snow yet feeling so light. The night has been amazing. We find our friends sitting off to the side on a mound of snow.

Chase stands as we get closer. "Hey, guys. You look like you've had fun. Gretchen here took another tumble, and her knee is hurting her pretty bad."

"Oh, no. I'm sorry, Gretchen. Why didn't you guys come get us?" I ask her.

Chase and Gretchen look at each other and both start to speak, but Gretchen backs off.

"I just thought it'd be best for her to rest, and I didn't want her to be alone," Chase says. "I figured I'd spot you two whenever you made your way over here."

We decide to call it a night at that point. It was fun, but it's time to head back.

Once we're back at Hunter's, I start to help Gretchen up the stairs when Hunter calls out to me.

"Jules, care to join me for a drink?"

I look back and forth between him and my best friend. I truly want to join him. I want to continue the evening. But I don't want to be a crappy friend. Plus, as much as I'm enjoying my time with him, for the sake of my heart, the smart choice is to end the evening.

"That sounds nice, but I'm beat. I think I'm just going to head to bed with Gretchen. Thanks again for tonight." I smile at him and turn back to help Gretchen.

Once we're in our room, Gretchen tries to get me to go back down. "I am *fine*. Go. You guys looked like you were having a good time tonight." She smiles at me.

"We were. But it's for the best if I stay up here. Remember, I thought this was going to be a girls' weekend." I look at her accusingly.

"Oh, get over it. You said we were fine. If we are, then you can't bring that up when you don't want to talk about what's *really* going on."

I go over to my bag and rummage through it, looking for my pajamas and toothbrush. "I don't know what you're talking about."

Gretchen's laughter stops my retreat into the bathroom. "The hell you don't. You keep everything and everyone in your life in these nice clean boxes you can check off and keep orderly. That isn't life, Jules. It sure as hell isn't living. Life is messy. Just like school, where most of our kids would rather fingerpaint than use a brush. Kids choose the messy way because it's more fun."

I stop avoiding her eyes and look at her. "Keep your voice down. I don't want the guys to hear us. Also, have you ever thought maybe I'm not most people? I enjoy using a paintbrush. I hate when I get the paint on me. Everyone isn't like you, Gretchen. I am doing my best, for me, and I'm sorry if you don't agree with it."

Her voice is softer when she says, "Jules, I love you. I grew up always wanting a sister, and I feel like I finally have one with you. I just want what's best for you. You don't have to be like me. But I don't think you are living, at all. If you want to keep with my silly analogy, I don't think you're painting at all. You're too busy obsessing over what to paint."

"We've talked about this. Hunter is great. It's just—"

"Stop. Don't bother finishing that. There is nothing else. He is great. You just won't allow it. And I'm sorry, but get over yourself and allow that stupendous heart of yours to *feel*—for someone over the age of six. My throat hurts with all this whispering. Hurry up and do what you need to in there. Once you're done, I'm going to take a bath and see if it helps with my knee."

I hurry into the bathroom and get ready for bed. I think about going back downstairs. But by the time Gretchen is done in the tub and comes out, I'm still sitting on my bed thinking about everything that happened today, my own worries controlling me and keeping me still.

WHEN I WAKE, the room is still dark. I roll over and search the floor for my phone. 9:47. I don't know the last time I slept so late. God bless blackout curtains. I try to see Gretchen across from me, letting my eyes adjust to the low light. I'm pretty sure she isn't there, so I turn on the flashlight on my phone. *Nope. No Gretchen.*

I make myself presentable before heading downstairs, where I find Hunter sitting at the kitchen table. The entire room is wood, walls, and ceiling. Tile covers the floors, though. Granite on the counters. And a copper hood interrupts the cabinetry. All of it is gorgeous. But my vision is drawn to the man with his back to me, looking at his tablet.

"Are you going to continue to stare or are you going to join me?" His voice is still raspy from sleep.

"Sorry." I walk over to the table. "I didn't want to bother you."

"You're never a bother." He moves out the chair next to him with his foot and motions for me to sit.

"Always with the perfect words. Thanks for the seat, but I'm going to make some tea first. Do you have any?"

"Far from having the perfect words." He gets up from his chair and moves across the room, around the island, and pulls out a basket from a cabinet. He clears his throat. "In fact, I am certain I lack the perfect words for what I'm about to say." He offers the basket to me, which is filled with different flavors of tea. "Chase and Gretchen are gone."

I drop the tea in my hand back into the basket. "What? What do you mean, *gone?*"

I can see the hesitation in him. "They won't be back. They're gone, gone. There's a note." He nods over to the far end of the island.

I pick up the note and gasp. *That little shit.* I am going to kill her.

*DEAR HUNTER AND JULES,*

*I'm sorry to do this. My knee is really bothering me. Chase offered to drive me back in my car, and I accepted. You two stay as planned. And Jules, I'm sure Hunter can bring you home tomorrow. Sorry.*

*~Gretchen*

"SHE BETTER BE HURT," I spit out like venom.

Laughter from Hunter fills the room. "I don't think this is a scheme. I will do whatever you want, though. I'd be thrilled for us to stay another night, but if you don't want to, it's not a problem and I can take you home now." He looks at me carefully.

I know what I want to say, but the fallout could be devastating. And, looking into his eyes right now, it appears he's silently pleading with me. I don't know if I have enough resolve to say I want to go home with any conviction. "What will we do? Just us."

A slow smile spreads on his face, up to his eyes. Like he knows I've already decided to stay. "Whatever you want."

# 13

# JULES

*G*od, I wish I could let him in. Gretchen made it sound so easy. But I'm so scared. When I started college, I tried dating. There were only so many dates that could end with me having a panic attack in the bathroom and the hostess coming to check on me because my date was wondering if I was okay.

One night, a friend dragged me to a party. I ended up running into a guy from my humanities class. We hung out at the party for a bit and ended up sleeping together. When he finished, he said, *"Maybe we can hang out again some other time."*

We ended up hooking up three other times that year. He never asked me out. Oddly enough, I was relieved. It was easy. I decided right then I would not date. At least not seriously. Dating leads to feelings, and feelings lead to making room in your life—your *heart*—for someone. Once that happens...control is lost, and things are sure to end in heartbreak and guilt.

Hunter grabs my hand, returning my focus to him. Damn, he wants an answer.

"It's just one more day. What the heck, let's stay," I decide.

"Great! What did you plan for you and Gretchen to do when

you thought it was just going to be the two of you here this weekend?" His smile takes over his whole face, and it's contagious.

My stomach flips. I'm happy, too. I think. I'm *something*—that's for sure. "Well, nothing really. We were going to have a lazy day. Movies. Gossip. Girl stuff. Nothing exciting and nothing I can see you being excited about."

"Did *girl stuff* comprise of touching each other? Because I'd absolutely be excited about that." He wiggles his eyebrows at me with the stupidest smirk.

I smack him on the shoulder. "Men. You're all pigs. Why does the idea of me and Gretchen touching each other do it for you?"

"What? Do you touch each other? No, I was saying since I'm your fill-in Gretchen, I get to take part in the touching." He wiggles his eyebrows again while grinning.

"The only touching you will be doing is to yourself."

"If that's your thing, I'm willing."

"Hunter. How did this veer so far off course? I'm going upstairs—alone—to change. Then we can figure out what to do when I come back down."

"Sounds good. But dress for being outdoors."

I go upstairs, unable to help the excitement taking root in me. I enjoy bantering with him. It's innocent enough. We'll just keep it at bantering. And I won't let myself think of the touching he brought up. *Nope. Not thinking about that.* Or remembering how turned on I got just from his kiss. Lord, what did I get myself into?

Wait. I didn't get myself into this. Gretchen did this to me. I enter the bunk room and look around for my bag. When I find it, there's a gift bag inside. I grab my phone to call Gretchen.

"Hello?" She greets me so cheerily.

"Gretch," I croon.

"I'm guessing you went to get dressed?"

"What did you do? You promised your departure wasn't planned."

"It wasn't. Honestly, when I packed it for you, I was hoping you'd sneak away with Hunter at some point during the weekend. Now it's even better because you have the whole house with just the two of you in it."

I peek in the bag again and blush. "I am not wearing this around Hunter. La Perla, though."

"Don't freak. My friend's sister works as a designer for them. She sends her stuff all the time. Some stuff fits her and some doesn't, so she gives away what doesn't. You and I are the same size in undergarments. Trust me, it's brand new. I just thought you could use it more than I could. So, it's yours."

I pull out the black underwire bra that has black floral lace over it. The black briefs fall out from being tucked inside the bra. They're Brazilian-cut briefs with tulle ruffle for the backside —and they are now the sexiest items I possess. "Well, thank you. I'm still not wearing them for Hunter. But I am not giving them back, either. They're all mine now."

"So, am I forgiven now for leaving?" Gretchen teases.

"I wish you were here so I could hug you. Call Chase and have him drive you back up here so I can." I start to laugh but stop when I hear her groan.

"Yeah, one trip stuck in a car with just us two is enough for my lifetime, thank you. I am not repeating that."

"What happened? You sound sad, like the ride was less than pleasant."

"Nothing to get into now. You go get dressed," she suggests. "I'm sure Hunter is waiting for you."

"Shoot, you're right. I better go, Gretch. But, we *will* be picking this back up later, okay? I want to hear about it."

"Okay. Have *fun*, Jules."

❦

102 | QUINN MILLER

TWENTY MINUTES LATER, I head back down to find Hunter. I hear his voice and follow it.

"Dude, not cool," he says. "She could have been pissed at me, and I had nothing to do with you two leaving. Yeah, she said we can stay. Dude, shut up. It's one day. I don't expect miracles. Ha. I'm not giving you shit. If I'm a lucky enough bastard to convince her to take a chance on me, that's on me, not because you stranded her here. Speaking of difficult women, how are things with you and Gretchen? Uh-huh. Really? I'm sorry, that sucks. Yeah, sounds good. Okay, I'll call you sometime next week."

I should feel guilty for hiding behind the wall to listen. But show me any female who would miss out on a conversation about themselves. Granted, I only heard one side of it, but it was enough.

I clear my throat as I walk into the kitchen, alerting Hunter of my presence. "I'm back and dressed for the day. What do you have in mind?"

A grin spreads as his eyes shine with happiness. "Snowshoeing. There are some incredible trails around here. I thought we could go check them out." He rocks back and forth on the heels of his feet, obviously excited. "By the look on your face, I'm guessing that's a crap idea."

"No." I shake my head. "I've always wanted to try snowshoeing. It just wasn't what I expected, that's all."

He comes up to me suddenly, bracing himself on the counter behind me. His proximity increases my heart rate to the point where I'm sure he can hear how loud and fast it is.

He just stands there looking at me. "What did you expect from me?" He looks briefly at my mouth before returning his gaze to my eyes. "Actually, don't tell me. I have to say though, hearing you had any expectation makes me exceedingly happy. Expectations mean you've been thinking about me. I like knowing you've been thinking about me. I can tell you I've been thinking about you. A lot. You ran from me, Jules. Not many people run from me, but you did. And I hated it. It's not about the chase, though. I hated it because I get along with a lot of people, but I rarely feel like I click with someone. And with you, I felt like we clicked. Plus, if I'm being honest, it's been over a month and I still want more of that mouth of yours."

"Hunter." I mean for his name to come out in a warning, but it comes out more like a moan.

By the way his eyes darken and his breathing stills for a moment, he heard it too. "Damn, I love hearing my name come out of your mouth. Especially when it comes out sexy and breathless. I promise if you let me, I'll make you breathless and you'll say a lot more of my name. But for now, let's do something safe. Like snowshoeing."

My breath is shallow. I don't know if any activity is safe with him. He pushes off the counter, grabs my hand, and heads toward the foyer while I trail behind him. His hand feels so satisfying in mine. The guy has barely touched me, and I already feel excited. I can't imagine what would happen if I gave him the green light.

We get all of our gear, and I follow Hunter toward the garage. He helps me as I climb into his truck. It makes me smile. I'm not sure why I find it so funny that he drives a truck. His black RAM 2500 doesn't fit the image of an investment firm owner. The truck is attractive; the inside is so smooth. Unlike the pickups I grew up with, I'm glad to see this one has a center console that prohibits me from moving any closer to him. It's a built-in buffer.

"What is that pretty mind of yours thinking?"

"I'm surprised you drive a truck."

"Why, do you not like it? We may need to just go back to Portland right now if you insult my truck."

His passion is amusing, though I can tell he's just teasing

me. "Calm down. I like your truck just fine. I just hear *investment firm* and think…"

I don't even know what I think. Perception is being clouded with reality. *Hunter.* That is what I think. He's taking up all the space in my brain, and I need to think of something—anything —else.

"You heard *investment firm* and thought, this guy is a tool. I bet he drives some slick sports car he has no idea how to handle. Am I right?"

I go to speak, but he places the pad of his index finger over my lips.

"Ah, it was. I can tell by the look in your eyes. Let me first clarify that I can *handle* anything—fast, slow, curves, you throw it at me, Jules, and I'll make sure it's handled. As for my truck…"

He runs his hand up and down the frame of the door. "I remember being a little boy, fascinated by pickup trucks. They just embodied power to me. I remember asking my dad if we could get one." He pulls back and shuts the door, then walks over to the driver's side.

As he starts the truck, I smile at him. The bit of his past he shares with me makes me picture my brother asking my dad something like that when he was little. Although Mitch probably would have asked for a three-wheeler instead of a truck.

"What did he say?" I tilt my head toward him.

With his chin on his shoulder, ready to reverse out of the garage, he appears as if he's contemplating what to say next as he slowly pulls out. I notice his knuckles turn white as his grip on the steering wheel intensifies.

"He slapped me across the face and told me I needed to worry about getting him a beer instead of wasting his time with dreaming." With that, he carefully starts the drive down his street.

I gasp, instantly moving to grasp his forearm. I've never

understood hurting a child. I've had to make calls to the Department of Child Services before because of bruising I saw on a student, and when asked, he told me his dad had hurt him.

I try to sound calm. "How old were you?" I can't imagine someone hurting a young Hunter with intent. He's so kind, so honest.

"When? The first time my dad struck me?" he asks, eyes on the road. "Ah, man. I grew up with him resenting me and letting me know it any chance he could. He was of the belief that his life was great until I came around. He hated me. But that's okay." He nods and gives me a small smile. "The feeling was mutual."

"Where is he now? He doesn't still work at the firm, right? You said it was your father's."

"Ah, close. You're thinking of my adoptive father, Benjamin. We can delve more into the inner workings of my family later. For now, I'll give you the shortened version. My semen donor was the piece of shit. Noah—that was his name—was not decent, and life settled that."

My hand covers my mouth in shock, my eyes widening. "Oh my God, Hunter. I am so sorry."

"Don't be. I'll just say, my own parents weren't very well equipped to be parents. Benjamin was a saint and took pity on me, took me in. He made sure I was educated and taught me the ins and outs of investing. In the right people, things, and places. It's almost coming up on a year since his passing. When he died, he left Steeple Investments—the firm he built—to me. I will forever be grateful to him."

He blows out a breath and offers me a smile. "Well, this all took a sad turn. How about we stop with all this and just go have some fun?"

When he pauses at a stop sign, he looks over at me and smiles, as if he didn't just rip a piece of himself out for me to look at.

With so much loss, I don't understand how he can pour himself out so freely. Isn't he scared of the pain? Doesn't he want to lessen the hurt?

He has shown me from the moment we met how open and honest of a person he is. It unnerves me, yet draws me in. And I'm noticing with every moment I spend with him, my rules are being forgotten more and more.

14

HUNTER

*T*he only sound for the rest of the ride is the noise my hand and stubble make the few times I rub my hands over my face. *Shit.* Why do I lose the ability to bullshit or hold back around her? I am not a standoffish person. I don't back away or pretend I don't come from where I do. But I also rarely dump it all out for someone else to deal with.

However, the way she's squished herself against the door, creating as much space between us as she can, makes me feel like I should have kept that information to myself.

I pull into the lot and put the truck in park. "Jules, are you okay?"

"Me? Yeah, I'm fine. Why?" She fidgets with some of the beads on her wrist. I don't know if it's the same bracelet I remember from our date or a different one.

I try to meet her gaze, but she avoids it. "Because you're as far from me as possible without being outside of this truck."

She takes a breath but says nothing.

So, instead of looking at her, I look out the windshield, taking in the beauty outside. "I know I gave you a lot of backstory there, and since then, you've been silent. Say something, please."

She turns her body to me. Her back is still against the door, but at least she's facing me now. "It was a lot. I just don't understand."

"Understand what? That my parents were messed up? Because let me tell you, they were. You don't understand how I went to live with Benjamin? How he gave me so much? What do you want to know? I want to tell you. I'm trying to be authentic right now. For you. But you need to tell me what you want. Let me give that to you. God, just let me in. Please."

"Why?"

"Damn, you love to be obscure, don't you?"

"Is that a question? I'm not trying to be ambiguous. I want to know why you want in so bad. We barely know each other. I don't feel like I've made the best impression on you. I don't understand—why me?" She looks scared.

I want to make her feel powerful. Right now, she looks breakable. I want to make her feel strong. I try to collect my thoughts so I don't word vomit all over her again. I spooked her again. My honesty didn't pay off. But my ability to filter myself around her has proven futile.

*How do you try to explain to someone how you feel?*

"People will fail you," I start. "Especially if you're always waiting for it. But people will also give you so much if you let them. It's a choice."

I tap my steering wheel and take a moment to control my breathing and inflection. "I've been shown time and time again that life can suck, *and* suck you down, if you let it. That's the key. I may be wrong, but I choose to hope."

I take a deep breath, and as I slowly let it out, I look at her. "As for *why* I want in. Why do I want you? Because, and let me be crystal clear here," I lace her fingers with mine, "I want you, Jules. You have all the power when it comes to us. But why? Because I want to witness all your joy, all your heart. I want to see you hope. You aren't ready yet, and I'm honestly not asking you to let me all the way in. Just don't shut me out. I want us to get to know each other. We can't do that if I hide and keep myself locked up, too. You are worth it. That's why."

Her breath stutters, and I can tell I won't get any more from her right now. And that's okay.

So, I smile at her and get out of the car, and then I walk around to her door. I stand out in the cold for a moment, seeing that she's still pressed against the door. I don't want to open it and have her dump out. Although I'm sure I'd catch her.

I wait. A minute later, she opens the door.

"Ready?" I try to sound as nonchalant as possible, the opposite of what I'm actually feeling.

"Yes. Let's go have some fun." She smiles, but it doesn't reach her eyes.

She's not letting me in, but she's not shutting me out, and I'll take it.

I interlock our fingers before bringing her hand to my lips, and I kiss her palm. It isn't much, but the smile she gives is enough. Plus, she didn't pull away, and that's all I need at the moment.

About an hour later, we're halfway around the lake. It's a perfect day.

We're stopped once again so she can take a photo. I learn that Jules loves to take photos with her phone. She said she couldn't wait to show her class what she did, to earn some points with them.

"How are you doing? Do you feel like you have the hang of it?" I ask.

She was nervous when we started, but I feel like she's settled in and has a groove now.

"After you fixed them and lined my foot up with the crampon

—and oh yeah, had me switch them so they were on the correct feet—so much better." She laughs and shakes her head.

"Hey, snowshoes can be confusing, especially for someone who's never done it. Give yourself some slack."

"All I know is I will never inwardly laugh at another student that walks around not noticing their shoes are on the wrong feet."

"Or you still will, but now it'll be because you're remembering today."

She laughs. The sound bounces off the surfaces around us, and it surrounds me in a snug hold that makes me smile. "So, you were saying how you became involved with Portland Social?"

"I take no credit for that. Chase did everything. He just needed some money."

"Some money, huh? I'm pretty sure he wouldn't be so cavalier about your contribution," she hints.

"He works his ass off for that place. He had a solid business plan. He tried getting the money from other places—banks—because he didn't want to mix business with friendship. But ultimately, he realized no one who could help him would care more about his vision than I would."

"That's amazing. I admire you. Both of you."

I feel her words all over. No one has ever complimented me like that.

She puts her gloved hand on my forearm. "Are you okay, Hunter?"

I look away for a moment, trying to think of what I want to say. "Your words mean a lot to me. I like talking to you, and the more we do talk, the more I'm impressed with you. So, hearing that, from *you*, means something to me. Thank you. I know you said you don't want anything between us, but I'd really like to at least be your friend, Jules."

She looks around, then at her snowshoes. She takes a deep

breath and raises her gaze to me. "Let me be transparent, because you have been with me. I haven't been out with anyone since our date, or for way too many months before that. I wasn't blowing you off that night, Hunter. I was blowing off dating in general. What I said was true. I don't do *commitment*. I could tell that night that things with us would never be simple. And I still feel like that's all I could handle. I knew if I slept with you, the sex wouldn't be light and easy. So, I ran. I ran because you scared me. Still do."

She takes a deep breath before continuing. "What you make me feel scares me. But I'm not an idiot. It isn't lost on me how special you are. You aren't someone that one *gets over*. I thought it was best to leave before anything really started." She gasps, as if her own words scare her.

I reach for her. "Damn these gloves," I say, ripping mine off. I place one hand on her waist and thread my fingers through her hair just below her ski hat with my other. "I don't want to scare you, Jules. I'm trying to let you lead this, but you can't say a word like *sex* when you're talking about us and expect me to ignore it."

I wait a bit to see if she pushes me away. When she doesn't, I take it as silent permission and lower my lips to hers. It takes all of my restraint to not make this kiss greedy. I try to keep it light and easy, for her.

When I pull away, her eyes are still closed. So I wait until she opens them and lets me get lost in her blue waters. "Since we're sharing how we imagine the sex between us will be, I can guarantee it won't be *light*. But, babe, it would be so easy and pleasing with us. Just one kiss tells me how exceptional it will be."

"Sledgehammer," she mutters.

"What?"

She shakes her head. "Nothing. I just didn't see you coming."

15

JULES

*hat the hell am I doing?* This is the opposite of what I should be doing. Curse this man and everything he is. He walks off so casually after that kiss and those words. Yet I'm still cemented here, trying to get a handle on my erratic heartbeat.

Hunter's earlier confession is still with me about how he came to be who he is. We both have faced such loss but handled it in vastly different ways. I don't know if I can be like him. I feel like all I do is hide. I don't hide to keep myself from others. I hide to keep them from me. Could I let myself feel something for him? Who am I kidding? I started feeling something that first night. But it's time for me to admit I want something more —and I want it with him.

It's easy to catch up to Hunter once I remember how to work my legs again. "What are you looking—"

"Shh."

I walk up behind him and see two deer just in front of him, drinking from the lake, which has yet to fully freeze over. The deer don't seem to care about us, or they simply haven't noticed they have company.

Hunter looks at me over his shoulder but doesn't say anything. I entwine our fingers and just allow myself to *feel*.

*How can such a simple touch feel so exhilarating?*

Hunter laughs and turns, spooking the deer.

"Shit, I didn't mean to say that out loud. Sorry." I bury my face in his chest in embarrassment.

"Stop apologizing around me. I like that you said it. I was already thinking about it myself. Sweetness, everything about you feels exhilarating. It scares me a bit that something as simple as you holding my hand feels this good. When we kiss, it's the best damn feeling I've ever experienced. It makes me wonder what something more would be like with you."

I look up into his hazel eyes, and they're gazing back at me. I swear they look darker than before. Without moving my eyes from him, I nod in agreement.

He moves a loose strand of hair behind my ear, and his finger traces down my neck, where I'm sure he feels my pulse racing.

"Going back to our conversation in the truck...why you? Because you make me want more. Hell, I never thought I'd have what I do now. Despite all the shit I went through, I'm a happy guy. I require little. I know that's easy for me to say when I don't want for much—*now*. But, I'm not talking about material things."

With his finger stroking just above the collar of my coat, I give him all my focus.

"I'm happy with the friends I keep, Jules. I can improve my mood by going outdoors and hiking. I've met and dated plenty of women. I've enjoyed my time with them, but when it fizzled out, I never wanted more. I don't push people to give me more. But damn it, I want to push you. I want the hand holding. I want to watch that smile appear when you kick my ass in some stupid game. I want to know if you always drink tea or if you sometimes have coffee. If you're a breakfast girl. I want to know more and I want more, and I am trying like hell to respect you and not push, but being around you makes my resolve slip. Because everything I find out about you makes you more and more amazing. That's why, Jules."

I'm so overwhelmed by his confession, I simply reach my hand out to take his and turn to continue on our path. Then, I look over to him. "I like tea in the morning. I don't always have time for breakfast, but I'm a huge fan of it. Gretchen makes fun of me for how often I make waffles for dinner."

The creases around his eyes from his enormous smile are sexy. To know I put that smile on his face is balm to my broken heart.

The rest of our outing goes smoothly. Since our kiss, I notice we reach for each other more. Just small touches. But it feels like a shift has occurred.

I don't think this would have happened had we just stayed in. I needed to get out of my own way and out of my head. I'm looking forward to seeing what the rest of the day now holds.

ONCE WE'RE BACK at his house, we linger in the foyer.

"I'm going to shower," he says. "Want to meet me back downstairs and we can enjoy a movie? I have Netflix, so we can stream something. Does that sound good?"

I smirk at him. "Are you asking me to *Netflix and chill* with you, Hunter?"

He smiles. I'm starting to crave those smiles.

"I'm just asking if you want to watch a movie, Jules. For now." He smirks and then walks toward his room.

I watch him walk down the hallway to his bedroom. As he does, he removes his shirt, and tosses it on a bench in the hallway. He never turns around, so I only see his back, but *holy hell*, the man takes excellent care of himself. I subconsciously feel the size of my stomach. I'm not in awful shape. But I'm not in his kind of shape, either. I push the thought away and run upstairs to shower.

As I go to get dressed after my shower, I grab a clean pair of underwear from my suitcase. But then the La Perla bag catches my eye. Not letting myself think too much about it, I grab the sexy bra and undies. *This doesn't mean he'll see it. I'm putting it on for me.* I don't even believe myself.

I look in the mirror before heading back down. I put joggers and a long sleeve T-shirt on. I apply minimal makeup and pull my hair back. But I don't miss how happy I look. I smile at my reflection and head downstairs.

"Hunter?" I call when I reach the last step.

"Walk past the kitchen," I faintly hear.

I turn down a small hallway past his room. When I find him, my mouth falls open. "You did not show us this on the tour." I look at the movie room, complete with plush seats, a full bar, and a snack bar. "You were holding out on us." I walk up to him and poke him in the side.

"Ouch." He grabs my finger and then laces our fingers. "I wasn't holding out on anything. I forgot about showing you this. I was a little nervous and thrown by you not knowing whose house you were staying in, and with whom." He points to the front of the room by the screen. "Over there are a bunch of blankets if you want to grab some while I grab drinks and snacks. What do you feel like eating—sweet or salty? And wine or beer?"

I look over his shoulder at the snacks. "I'll have some chocolate-covered pretzels, please."

He smiles at my combination of choices.

"And for right now, I'm good with water. I'll fall asleep if I drink," I admit.

I'll never remember the movie we're watching. Years from now, when I look back on this weekend, it won't stand out to me. What I will remember is how close he was. How good he smelled. How I could feel the heat coming off him. How calm my body felt when I got up enough nerve to rest my head on his shoulder. The smiles I couldn't help every time he kissed the top of my head. How the simple back-and-forth swipe of his thumb on my knee felt—even through my pants—between my legs and made me squirm. That is what I will remember.

I am so damn turned on. I hope he'll kiss me again. I hope he won't stop with just a kiss. But I know that won't happen. He said as much. He's handing over all the control to me.

As the movie ends, I shift on the couch, totally forgetting about my water resting between us, now spilled. "God, I am so sorry."

"Jules, it's just water. No worries."

"But I've soaked your couch and you." I stand, all flustered.

Hunter stands too, then puts his hands on my shoulders. "Like I said, it's just water. I barely got any on me, but I'm afraid you weren't so lucky."

I look down and the right side of my pants is soaked; as is the bottom of my shirt. I look up at him from under my lashes. I don't think he even realizes he's rubbing my shoulders. This is probably the dumbest choice I could make, but I don't care how I'll feel tomorrow.

"I'll be right back." But I don't head upstairs. I head toward the hall bath, and I grab his shirt off the bench.

Right now, I just want to know how all-encompassing it will feel to be with him.

# 16

## HUNTER

\

*K*nowing a bathroom door is the only thing keeping us apart is driving me crazy. I don't know what she's doing in there. I figured she was going to change, but she didn't head upstairs. With every little noise, I think she's coming out.

*God, man. Calm the fuck down.* She could come out and nothing would happen.

*Fuck. I hope something happens.*

I look out the back windows. The sun set hours ago. Finally, I hear the click of the door handle. I don't turn around, saying a silent prayer for restraint. I find her reflection in the dark windows right away, and I am screwed. I have no control left. If she doesn't want this, I'll be crushed.

I turn, taking in all that's in front of me now. She stands there, bewitching me in the shirt I discarded before my shower. She is gorgeous. Damn, standing there in only my shirt...her gorgeous legs bare...she's the sexiest woman I've ever seen or dreamed of.

"You are the most alluring woman," I say, and I mean it. "I

think you forgot some of your outfit, though." I offer her a cocky smirk.

She's torturing me and enjoying it, but I love seeing this side of her. All I can think about right now is having those legs wrapped around me.

"Really?" She looks down at her bare legs, running her hands down to the bottom of my shirt she has on. She pulls one side of it up, exposing black underwear and one black lace covered breast.

My athletic pants do shit for hiding how hard she's making me. Her stare beholds me.

"Huh, oh well. I'm comfortable like this. Does it make you uncomfortable, Hunter?" Jules gazes at me innocently, knowing full well she's anything but innocent in this moment. She drops her hold on my shirt she's wearing and it once again falls to the tops of her thighs.

To make matters worse, she casually walks across the room, not to me, but to the kitchen. Without hesitation, I follow her.

As she stretches to reach a glass in the cabinet, the shirt rises, exposing her round ass. I take the time to appreciate every curve. I'm not aware if the growl I feel in my throat actually comes out or not, but seeing as she looks at me over her right shoulder, batting her eyelashes with a smirk, I'm guessing it did.

Before I can think about it, my body goes on autopilot, and I walk up behind her. Without touching her, both my arms go against the cold granite. I feel like I'm on fire, and the coolness is of little help.

As I cage her in, her body is perfectly lined up with mine. She lowers herself from the balls of her feet, rubbing against me as she goes. She has to feel how turned on she's making me.

"Fuck. You're driving me insane. I'm giving you an out, Jules. You tell me now that you don't want this, and I'll walk away. I might need to jerk off twice, but I'll leave you alone. You told me once you didn't see yourself with me. If that hasn't changed,

I will respect that. But tell me now. Because I need you, and once I touch you, I won't be able to stop."

Then, I wait. I count to five because I'm not a patient man right now, and I don't want to give her too much time to over-think this.

She makes no effort to speak, but she takes the smallest step back—pressing her back into the front of me—and does a figure-eight with her hips.

That's all it takes.

I move her hair to one shoulder, going to her right ear. "You are so damn seductive. This shirt is yours now. If I ever wore it again, I'd instantly get hard thinking of you in this moment. You are ruining me."

"Is that bad?" Her breath comes out in a quick burst, making her chest rise and fall. She turns her head slightly, locking gazes with me.

I move my hands to her hips and squeeze, then crawl up her body, under the shirt, until I cup her breasts. I feel the friction of the lace rub against my palms and her nipples, but it isn't enough. I need to feel her skin on mine.

I grab the hem of her shirt and swiftly move it up her body and toss it somewhere on the floor. I unhook her bra and toss it in the same direction. My hands go right back to her breasts, but this time, nothing is between us.

I tease her nipples, and she once again presses against me, her head falling back against my chest. A moan escapes her lips.

Turning around, she stands in front of me in only her under-wear. I take my time slowly moving it down her body. As my gaze makes its way back up to her face, she has the biggest grin on.

"See something you like, Hunter?" Her eyes drop to my hard-as-steel cock tenting my athletic pants, and she bites her bottom lip before looking into my eyes. She's well aware of how she's affecting me.

"Damn straight I do." My mouth slams down on hers. This isn't a patient, sweet kiss like our first one was. It isn't a light and easy kiss like the kind we shared at the lake.

In this one, we are both hungry.

My one hand cups the back of her head, my fingers in her hair. My other hand rests on her hip and grips her close to me.

Jules will be the end of me. And I'm ready.

Both of my hands go to her ass and I lift her up. Her legs automatically wrap around my waist, and she grinds against me.

"Sweetness, you have to stop doing that or I won't make it to the bedroom. I will end up laying you out right here on the granite island and take you."

"And that's bad, why?"

"I've thought about how this would go too many times. I want to be able to take my time. I *need* to take my time with you. I want to worship this insane body. In. A. Bed."

"I won't move again till you tell me to."

Without further words, I walk us to my room. I lay her down on my bed, kissing my way up her leg from her knee to her inner thigh.

"What are you doing?" She reaches down, trying to block me.

"If you don't know, then I'm not doing a very sufficient job."

She smiles shyly. "I...I mean, it's just...I've never..."

"Shit, has no one ever done this?" I run my hand over my jaw. *Is she for real?*

"No. No one has ever cared to take the time." Her hands go to cover her face, and she blushes from embarrassment with her confession.

I grab her wrists and move her hands. "Thank Christ. You have been with idiots, Jules. Tonight, I'm going to show you the way you deserve to feel." With that, I flick my tongue against her clit.

She arches off the bed, and I have to put my left hand on her abdomen to keep her still. Between sucking and flicking my tongue, I can tell she's already getting close to coming.

I need to make sure she comes at least once before we have sex. I insert two fingers inside, curving them up to hit her G-spot. Between that and my mouth on her, I feel her start to pulse.

17

## JULES

"*D*amn, that feels wonderful. Ahh, shit—ah—please, please, Hunter."

He leaves his fingers in me in a come-hither motion and takes his gloriously talented mouth off me, briefly. "Please what, beautiful?"

"Let me...let me come, please."

It starts in my stomach. A flutter. My toes and fingers go numb. My one hand clenches around the bedsheet while the other goes to Hunter's head, my fingers threading through his hair.

"Oh my God. Oh, Hunter, that feels so good. Right there. I'm going to—"

The most glorious orgasm takes over my body. Hunter doesn't stop his delicious assault on my body until I come down, my breath finally calming.

"That was the best thing I've ever seen," he says.

"That's encouraging. Because that was by far the best thing I've ever felt." I lift my head up to see the cockiest grin on Hunter's face. We haven't even gotten around to having sex, and he's already better than anyone else I've been with. His ego doesn't need the boost, but I can't lie right now. "Thank you." And that grin gets even bigger.

"Are you on birth control?" Hunter asks as he kisses his way up my body.

"Yeah, but if you have a condom, I'd rather be too careful than sorry. Is that okay?"

He stops and looks at me—really looks at me. "Sweetness, don't you dare ever worry about telling me what you want. I'm the lucky one right now and will do whatever you want."

He quickly gets up from the bed and grabs a condom from his bedside drawer. I watch as he rolls it on, over his impressive size. He catches me watching and I'm treated to another of his sexy smirks. As he moves between my legs and lines up, he locks his gaze onto mine once again, silently asking if I'm okay with this.

As I bite my lip, I give a slight nod, and Hunter fills me in one thrust.

"Damn, you feel so good. You're so tight, Jules. Are you sure I'm not hurting you?"

"No, you feel incredible. But Hunter, move, please." And he does.

The man has skills I have never experienced. The way he thrusts in and out, hitting me inside in just the perfect spot. I can feel his hands everywhere. It's like he's trying to memorize my body. I can already feel my body start toward bliss again. I've never orgasmed more than once.

I try to focus on him, but the feeling is too much and my eyelids close. My hands explore everything I can touch. I feel his muscles contract as he moves above me. He reaches between us and finds my clit, circling it.

"Open your eyes." It isn't a demand. More of a plea.

I do, and then I'm struck by the emotion I see in his gaze. "Shit. Oh, right there. God, that feels—*ah*, I'm coming, Hunter."

Hunter follows right behind me, with my name on his lips.

Both of us are breathing hard, and I can still feel my muscles involuntarily contracting around him.

"Are you trying to make me hard again? Jules, you are incredible. You feel incredible. Watching you climax might be the best sight I have ever seen. And there is my second favorite sight. You're blushing, beautiful."

I feel it on my face, radiating down my chest. This man undoes me.

"Hey now, no getting embarrassed. I love how responsive you are to me. Are you kidding? You make me feel like there's no one else for you."

And in that moment, I am the one ruined. Because I know nothing will ever feel this unbelievable. No one will ever fit me like this.

WAKING up to a new day hasn't always been my favorite. The first few months after the accident, I hated waking up. It was like reliving the loss of them all over again, every day. Because at night, I'd dream. And in my dreams, they'd both be there.

In my dreams, our time played out how I could control it. In my dreams, my brother was so happy Matt and I got together. In my dreams, I never lost either one of them.

After some time passed, I dreamed less and less about them. It made me feel guilty. It made me feel like, somehow, I was moving on without them. I hated sleep, and I tried to avoid it.

Once I started college, I slept normal hours again. I tried to push aside the guilt. But all the built up guilt came crashing into me when I slept with someone. I never fell asleep in someone's arms. Not in Matt's, or anyone else's I'd slept with since.

This morning I woke up warm, engulfed in arms and legs.

I smile and move back to cuddle closer against him. I take a moment to check in with myself. To allow myself to feel. I prepare for the waves of guilt to crash over me. But I don't feel any. I feel good. I feel better than good.

My body is sore from being well used. I feel...*happy*. I try stretching, wiggling my butt, just trying to move a bit. A hand clamps down on my hip—a hand attached to the most delicious man.

"Please stop thinking so much," Hunter says. "I can hear your brain from here. No regrets, okay? Also, unless you want me to take you again, please stop moving that fine ass against me. I have no willpower against it."

"Ah, an ass man, are you?" I turn to my other side to look at him. His hand moves down to grab my butt. "And I don't regret a thing about last night." I kiss him along his jaw. "Or the two other times that were technically today."

After our first time, we showered to clean up. We were only thinking of the environment by showering together. I wasn't about to complain when Hunter dropped to his knees and put my left leg over his shoulder while he made me come.

After our shower, he dried me off with a towel, then picked me up and carried me to bed. We fell asleep wrapped around each other. At some point in the middle of the night, I woke him with kisses down his abdomen. I planned on repaying my shower orgasm, but he said he needed to be inside me. I wasn't about to argue with the man. And now, as we touch, talk, and tease, I can feel him getting hard for round four.

"I'm an everything man when it comes to you." He runs his hand down my side. "Tell me the story of this. It's beautiful." His fingertip traces lightly over the butterfly tattoo on my ribs.

I tense because I don't want to talk about it. So, I wrap my leg around his hip, and by his sharp intake of air, I can tell Hunter feels how wet I am for him.

"Damn, you're trying to kill me. I'm not complaining about it, though. There'd be no better way to go." He moves up my body, touching me everywhere.

I stretch, opening his nightstand drawer for a condom before rolling it on him. I lower myself onto him, our gazes locked on the other's. Being with him makes me feel powerful, surrendered, and in control all at once. It makes no sense, but it's addicting. I am addicted to Hunter. Maybe I will worry about that later. But right now? No.

"Stop thinking and just feel. You feel so extraordinary around me. So tight."

All thought stops, and I allow all of him and our sounds to encompass me, and I feel it all.

# 18

## JULES

*a* s we head back to Portland later in the day, I feel like an idiot with my constant smile. Hunter keeps touching me when he can take a hand off the wheel. We haven't talked about what comes next.

"You're the first guy I've ever slept with." His head quickly swivels to look at me. "Wait...not sex. I wasn't a virgin. I just never stayed around afterward to fall asleep with anyone before. Not that there have been *so* many men. Shit. I'm stopping now. Sorry."

His laughter fills the cab of the truck. "Breathe, Jules. We're good. We are epic together. Last night was incredible, and this morning. This is new for us both. So, stop beating yourself up for your confessions. I love your awkward verbal diarrhea."

"You make it sound so titillating." I cover my face with my hands. I don't know why I'm so awkward around him some-times. I just open my mouth and all these words pour out of me.

He pulls the truck over into a Dairy Queen parking lot. "Look at me. I love that I can experience firsts with you, whether it's your first, my first, or our first. Thank you for not leaving last night and going to your own room. Falling asleep with my arms around you was everything." He reaches for my hand, brings it to his mouth, and places a sweet kiss on the inside of my wrist.

"That's what scares me. I never even thought to leave your bed last night. I don't want to move too fast. I can't, okay?" I can see him tense. "I am not backtracking. I told you, no regrets. I promise. But this is new for me. So just be patient, please."

"We can take this as slow as you want. As long as we're together. Just don't run from me again, okay? I like this, Jules. I like you. I just want you to give us a chance to figure out what it can be. Everything about you fascinates me."

He smiles at me, crinkling the skin around his eyes. "And for your information, this is all new for me too. I've never had anyone I was serious about in my life. But just know, Jules, I am yours. I am not seeing anyone else. And you are mine. Agreed?"

I nod. "Okay. Thank you, Hunter." I bite the inside of my cheek, trying to hide my smile. This feeling is incredible, and I don't want it to go away.

"OH MY GOD, you two make me sick," Gretchen bellows as she comes into my classroom.

She's carrying a large vase of purple tulips. They're beautiful. And also, my favorite flower.

"What is that?" I look wide-eyed at the beautiful arrangement.

"Um, they're flowers, honey. Even your students know that. Too bad they were dismissed already or they could have clued you in," Gretchen teases, winking at me.

"I see that they're flowers, but for me? From who?"

"Oh, I don't know. Happen to sleep with any rich, hot, kind, and totally-into-you guys recently?"

"Gretchen." Heat crawls up my chest and face.

*Did Hunter send me flowers?* And he sent them to my work.

My dad always said, *"A good guy sends flowers; a smart man sends them to your work where it can make all the other women around you jealous."*

By the way Gretchen is looking at my flowers, I'd say my dad is a wise man.

"I can't believe he did this," I say.

"Yeah, I mean, how much more perfect does this man get? It's kind of sickening. You've been to his place. Are there dead bodies hidden in the freezer or anything? Please tell me he has flaws."

"Nope, no dead bodies. Just incredible sex, in every square inch of his house. And everyone has flaws."

I haven't quite figured out what Hunter's flaws are, but trust me, his ability to make me orgasm is not one of them. Gretchen has been grouchy lately, though. So I am not sharing that tidbit.

"Now you're just being rude, rubbing in your fabulous love-making you have with the delectable Mr. Peterson." She crosses her arms and pouts.

I know Gretchen is kidding, but it's been a few weeks now of her passive aggressive comments. At first, I thought maybe she wasn't happy for me. But she's since assured me that she is, so I don't know what it could be.

"Gretchen, what's going on? I know you aren't *this* mad at me for getting flowers. This has been going on for a while now. Please tell me what's up."

"Ugh, I'm sorry. I'm not trying to make you feel bad about being happy. I'm so glad you got out of your own way and are seeing Hunter. Maybe it's just all the stress leading up to winter break. I'm tired. There's a lot going on in my head these days. Nothing to worry about. I'll work on being less bitchy—truly. I'll let you go so you can get out of here. Are you going home tonight or going to Hunter's again?" She walks over by my cubbies and looks out the windows.

"Hunter has a late meeting tonight, so I was planning on going home. Will you be there?"

Before she responds, my classroom phone—which is right next to her—rings.

"I need to text Hunter real quick to thank him for the flowers. Can you grab that, please?" It's most likely our school secretary, and since Gretchen and I are still here past contract hours, it shouldn't be anything important.

**Me**: I got the prettiest flowers delivered to my work today. Excellent job making the female staff here jealous. I love them. Thank you. Did I tell you my favorite flowers are tulips or did you just get lucky?

**Hunter**: When we were food shopping the other day, you saw some tulips and made a comment about how they were your favorite. I know purple is your favorite color, so I went with that. I'm sorry I can't see you tonight. I will make it up to you tomorrow.

I smile, unable to believe he remembered some off-the-cuff remark and picked up on my favorite color.

"Oh, Lord. Wipe that grin off your face," Gretchen says. "We've been summoned."

"Really? Why?"

"Linda just said for us both to come to the office to pick up a delivery. Not sure what it is." Gretchen shrugs and moves to wait for me by the door.

We enter the office from the hallway door, and the whole lobby is filled with boxes. So many boxes.

"What is all of this?" I look around and there are boxes upon boxes, all stacked.

"This is for you two. Your donor projects were both fully funded. You now have a whole class set of new Chromebooks. One of you sure made an impression on someone…"

I completely forgot about my request for Chromebooks I put in before we headed up to the mountain.

Gretchen gasps next to me. "Mine too?"

Linda looks at both of us. "Yes, yours too. You really don't know who did this? It was one donor. I was sure at least one of you would have an inkling."

"You don't think...do you?" Gretchen looks at me wide-eyed, seemingly speechless over our new tech and what it would mean for our kids.

"I don't think what?" I ask, seriously stumped.

"Come on, Jules. Hunter."

"What? No. That's crazy."

She tilts her head. "Who else in our lives has enough funds to do something like this?" She stares at me expectantly, like she's waiting for me to run through each of the parents in our classes and try to so much as think of another possibility.

"Oh my God."

"Jules, ask him. This is crazy. Don't get me wrong, it's crazy good. But why would he fund mine too?"

As she's talking, I quickly send him another text.

**Me**: Sorry for the bother. Any chance you sent me more than some flowers today? I'm in a sea of Chromebooks. So is Gretchen. Did you do this?

"I don't know," I tell her. "I just texted to ask him. Man, will I feel stupid if it wasn't him." My cell vibrates in my hand.

**Hunter**: Don't be mad. The company does things like this a lot, especially for Title One schools. I'm just glad we could help the kids out.

**Hunter**: As for Gretchen, I owed her for stranding you on the mountain that weekend. I will always be indebted.

I shake my head. *This man.*

"GRETCHEN?" I call. "I'm home, and I have dinner."

"Bedroom," she yells back. "I'll be out in a few."

I put the takeout on the butcher block island in our kitchen. I can't help the grin as I look at my flowers in the center. On a whim, I take a pic and send it to my mom.

**Me:** Tell Dad he was right. Smart men do send flowers to your work. All my coworkers were swooning. Miss you guys. I'm excited to see you.

In truth, I can't decide how to feel about going back home for Christmas.

Anytime I'm back in Redmond, memories of Mitch and Matt consume me. My parents always host Christmas dinner at their house with the Gregory family. Being around Matt's parents makes me uneasy. They don't know that we were dating, or that the only reason their son was in that car that night was because of me. Plus, dinner with them also means dinner with Eric. That, I am not looking forward to.

Regardless, I am excited to see my parents. Just then, my phone vibrates. I find a text from my mom.

**Mom:** Trying to bury the lead, honey. Who is sending you flowers??? Inquiring minds want to know.

I text her back, telling her a little about Hunter and promising to share more once I'm home for Christmas.

Gretchen walks in and pulls out one of our stools while I put my phone down and grab us some plates.

"Are you looking forward to going home to Redmond?"

"I am, but I'm going to miss Hunter. It sucks." I sit down next to her. I pass her salad to her, put mine in front of me, and put the breadsticks between us.

"Who are you and what have you done to my roommate? She's about five-six, cute, and refuses to seriously date anyone."

"Ha. So funny. I'm still me. I'm just trying a fresh approach to things."

"Well, keep it up. I like seeing you like this." She waves her fork around in a circle, pointing the tines at me.

I smile at her. "What, happy?"

"More like in love."

After inhaling a piece of the breadstick I was chewing, I start to cough. Gretchen pats my back. "What are you talking about? Gretch, no one said anything about *love*."

She holds up her hands. "Fine. You might not be there yet, but you are falling. And no one can blame you for it."

My food forgotten, I hear her words on a loop in my head. *Is she right? Am I falling for Hunter?* I might not have been the first to recognize it, but that doesn't make it any less true.

I *am* falling.

# 19

# JULES

The Christmas before Mitch's accident was my favorite one. Sadly, it was also our last. He was a junior in high school and had been going on college visits since the summer. I always asked him his thoughts after each trip and tried to be as positive as I could. But he knew me better than anyone. He was leaving me, and I wasn't ready. Little did I know how vast that void I feared would turn out to be.

But that Christmas, Mitch made me a photo album. Usually, it was me with the sentimental gift-giving, but that year I gave him a gift card to Burgerville. It was his favorite fast food. I was trying to be practical.

When I opened the photo album he'd created online, my eyes flooded. On each page, he listed a distinct memory, along with a reason why he loved me. The title of the album was: *Why Jules Is The Best Sister EVER.*

The last page simply stated: *To Be Continued...*

The day of his memorial, I ripped that last page out and burned it.

I'd never get more memories with Mitch.

It wasn't my parents' fault that the holiday wasn't as joyous for me after that. But it still hurt to be there.

It's why, even though I was given two weeks off, I would only be in Redmond for three days.

I arrived this early this morning—Christmas—and will go back to Portland on the twenty-eighth. I wish I could handle a longer visit, but I'm not that strong.

"Okay, I let you settle in. All of our presents have been opened. Food is all prepped. Now tell me about the boy."

I'm currently cuddled up beside my mom on the couch under the big blanket she has in the family room. We've only just sat down, with cups of warm cider and a plate of cookies. With the remote still in my hand after turning on a Hallmark Christmas movie, I hit pause and turn to my mom. "Well, he isn't a boy. His name is Hunter and he's a little older than me. He owns an investment firm in Portland. We met in the fall at a bar his friend owns."

"Thank you for the dossier. I acknowledge I'm ancient in your eyes, but I can Google, you know."

"Oh my Lord, Mother. You Googled him? How? When? Why?"

She calmly takes a sip of her hot cider before answering me, like it's no big deal that she cyberstalked the guy I'm dating. "I typed his name into the search bar. Easy."

"How did you know his full name?"

She picks up her cell from her lap and unlocks it. A minute later, she swivels her phone around for me to see, our text thread pulled up. Clear as day, I see I texted her his full name. I look at the date, noticing it was sent on the last day of school before break. I look at her with my eyebrows raised.

"Hey, it's not my fault I asked you about him when you were in party mode with a bunch of sugar-crazed kids."

"You struck when you knew I was weak is what you did." If

she wasn't such a genius, I'd be irritated. But all I could do was laugh at her skills.

"As for the *why*, because I love you. And this boy—sorry, *man*—is the first one you've ever talked to me about. He is impressive, Jules. I'm not referring to his financials. I mean, that is staggering, but I found so many articles mentioning his philanthropic side. He seems kindhearted."

My cheeks heat at my mom's description. Hunter really is so giving. "You remember my donor project for Chromebooks for my classroom?" I bite my lip before sharing with my mom, trying to tone down my smile. "He sponsored the whole thing. Gretchen's classroom, too. I had no idea. The boxes just showed up one day."

She puts her hand on my knee and squeezes. "That's amazing. It sounds like he must think you're pretty special too if he would do something like that."

I nod my head.

"I expect you'll be bringing him to your dad's party."

I groan. My mom's throwing my dad a fiftieth birthday party. I was told months ago it'd require me to be here for a long weekend and to plan accordingly. "Mom, there's no guarantee we'll even be together still by the time the party happens. Let's not get ahead of ourselves."

"You don't see yourself staying with him by then?"

"I don't know. And that's my point. This is new for me, you know that. I just want to be smart."

"Well, sweetie, you are smart. Just make sure you also have faith." She takes the remote from my hand and plays the movie.

After our movie, I rush upstairs. I have about an hour to get ready for dinner.

After I finish, I grab the banister, taking one more steadying breath before descending the stairs. The Gregory family must already be here. I can hear Eric's booming voice coming from the front room.

At the bottom of the stairs, I quickly turn left, avoiding where the voices are coming from and heading toward the kitchen where I'm sure I'll find my mom.

"How can I help?" I ask as I open the cabinet to grab a wine glass. "Wine?"

"Things are all set and the prime rib is cooking, so I think we're good. I'd love a glass. Did you say hi to Eric? He's out there watching basketball with your dad."

As I uncork the wine, I pause for a second. I put the bottle down and hear my mom sigh. I turn to look at her.

"Don't be mad. I didn't tell you sooner because I knew you wouldn't come if it would be just the four of us. Paula and Bill went on a cruise after hearing what a wonderful time your father and I had when we went on ours. Eric would have been alone, so of course I told him he should still come."

Before I can say anything, an arm wraps around me, pulling me back against solid muscle in an awkward hug.

"There's my girl."

I roll my eyes and pat Eric's arm. "I am not your girl." My mom glares at me, so I plaster on a smile while wiggling out of his hold. "But hello, Eric."

The evening turns out to be uneventful, thankfully. Eric and my dad watch the basketball game and my mom and I mostly stay in the kitchen, catching up and looking at pictures from their cruise.

After dinner, Eric joins my dad in the kitchen to wash all the dishes, and I excuse myself out back for a moment to myself.

That is, until I hear the door slide open.

Eric emerges from my house carrying two tulip-shaped glasses with what I assume have whiskey in them. Eric bends slightly, handing me one. "You didn't touch your wine, so I brought you out some of your dad's Green Spot." He holds up his now empty hand. "I swear he okayed it before I poured any."

Despite the smile he's giving me, I just stare at him. He no longer reminds me of Matt. But I wonder what Matt would look like now if things had been different. Eric has changed so much in the last seven years. His jawline is now hard, which I'm sure serves him well when having to be stern at work.

"How's work going?" I ask him.

"Good. I mean, it's Redmond. Theft is up but so is the population, so, still low overall." He takes a sip of his whiskey. "Enough of the polite talk like we're strangers. How are you? Your mom says there's a guy."

I smile at the mention of Hunter. We've texted a few times since I got here, and he's calling me later tonight. "Don't worry, officer. My mother has already looked into him. Apparently, she knows how to cyberstalk." I laugh, trying to lighten the awkwardness in the air.

"Yeah, that was my doing. I ran into her while grocery shopping and commented on the flowers in her cart. She couldn't hide her excitement in sharing how you had your own flowers delivered. I told her she should look the guy up. Make sure he's worthy of our Jules." The words are kind, but he says it all with a bit of contempt in his voice.

We just look at each other for a moment. I can see the tic in his jaw. "Thanks for the concern, Eric. But I'm a big girl and can handle my own life."

"Your life is supposed to be back here. Your Portland adventure has gone on long enough. The last time you were home, I could tell you were considering coming back. Now some rich guy in a suit chases after you and you toss out all your own plans?"

Green Spot is a sipping whiskey. But right now, I pound it, not giving it the time it deserves. I need the moment the burn down my throat makes me take. "Coming back here hasn't been in my plan since high school. I stayed to make sure they were okay." I point to my parents' house. "It was time for me to go. I understand you enjoy being here, but I don't. There's too much history, and it's suffocating for me. Portland isn't an adventure, or experiment. I have a life there—a good one. And who I date is none of your business. It never has been."

I walk away, shaking from the adrenaline. I head inside and up to my bedroom, where I pull out my phone. Hunter will be calling in about an hour, but I need to hear his voice now. In fact, I feel like I need to see his face, so I choose to video chat him instead.

I can't suppress the grin when I see his face appear on the screen. "Hey."

"Hello, gorgeous. Merry Christmas."

I say nothing for a moment. I just take my time looking at every inch of him I can see. Hunter is spending Christmas in Jackson Hole, Wyoming with Chase and some other buddies.

"Merry Christmas. You look handsome but drunk."

"I am not drunk, but I have had a few." He chuckles, but then just looks at me for a moment. "I wish you were here."

I laugh at how perfectly *Hunter* he is, cutting right through the bullshit. "I wish we were together too, but at least we can see each other."

"Don't laugh at me. I'm being serious. I miss those eyes. Video calls don't do those eyes justice." He rubs his hand over his face. "You're amazing, Jules."

"Hunter." It comes out like a moan. I bite my lip. There's still so much about me—about my past—I haven't shared with him. This thing with us is still new; at least that's what I keep telling myself when I avoid sharing certain things with him.

"You make me so fucking happy, Jules."

We both just stare at each other again, this time with the goofiest grins on our faces. I keep expecting panic to settle in, telling me to run. But it hasn't. All I feel is happiness.

"You make me happy too, Hunter."

I love the grin he gives me. I hope I am the only one to make him this happy and to see this particular grin. I feel like it heals a little something in me.

We talk for a bit until he has to go. We wish each other goodnight and sweet dreams. I do sleep well, for I dream of him.

"DAD ALREADY PUT your bag in your car. Promise to call me when you get back to Portland so I know you make it safely?" my mom says.

It isn't lost on me that she still doesn't call Portland my home. Eric isn't the only one that hopes I'll return here for good. I pull my mom in for a hug. "I promise I'll call when I get home."

"This will always be your home, lady. Oh, and don't forget, I expect you *and* Hunter at your dad's party."

I huff out a breath. With the way she's looking at me, there's no point in trying to argue. "How about I promise to invite him? I can't *make* him come."

She nods. Then, after one last hug from each of my parents, I get behind the wheel.

Hunter will be back in town today too, and I'm hoping I'll get to see him tonight.

The moment I leave Redmond city limits, I feel my lungs fill with air. During the ride home, I compartmentalize my two worlds—Portland and Redmond. I realize I've just put a clock on the merging of the two.

My dad's party is less than two months away. That gives me less than two months to work up the nerve to talk to Hunter about certain things I haven't shared with him. *Plenty of time.*

# 20

# JULES

*T*urns out, that *plenty of time* I had dwindled quickly. As promised, I asked Hunter to come along for the trip to my dad's party, and now, we're in the car on the way there.

"Okay, we have a three-hour drive. Do you want to listen to the playlist I made? Or are you an audiobook person?" He looks at me with so much excitement in his eyes. He packed snacks and put together a playlist just for the drive.

I, however, am dreading it. I've had plenty of time—more if you count since the first time we met—to tell him certain details about my life. But I keep pushing it off. Telling him about my past would open wounds I'm not sure have ever healed.

Gretchen kept pushing me lately to tell Hunter about the accident that colored my past. Every time I thought I was ready to, I just couldn't. Sometimes it felt like there were no words adequate enough to explain the void. Other times, I worried it would somehow change how Hunter saw me. Like I would appear weaker, more fragile.

So, I didn't even try. There was no way I could share a portion of my past without divulging everything.

At his company's holiday party, there were twenty question

cards at every table to encourage socializing. One of Hunter's coworkers asked me a question when it was my turn. *"Name a place that has changed you, and why."*

My mind instantly went to Haystack Reservoir, and the memories I made there with Matt. I must have looked stricken, because that sweet woman holding the card became so concerned.

"Oh, honey, you're shaking. Hunter, let's get her outside for some fresh air."

I was grateful for the escape, but I could see the questions in Hunter's eyes. He held off on asking until later that night when we were in bed back at his house.

There, he asked me if I wanted to talk about it. He didn't push when I said no. But the look in his eyes came back, then and now.

I think he knows I'm hiding something. And here we are, just hours from arriving at my parents' house, with my worlds about to crash together.

"Jules, did you hear me?"

"Sorry. Usually, I do an audiobook," I confess. "But with you, I'd say music. First, though...I want to talk to you about something."

I grab my water bottle and drink for a solid thirty seconds. My mouth is so dry. And I'm stalling.

As I put my water bottle in the cup holder, a yawn takes over. I hardly slept last night. I was too anxious about this weekend.

"Sure. Let's just get on the road and then we can talk," he says. "The weather isn't the best, so I just want to get through town. Sound good?"

I nod, and he picks up my hand and kisses it before starting my car. His truck is having some maintenance done on it, so we're taking my car, but he offered to drive.

"It means a lot to me that you asked me to join you," he adds, and I can hear the happiness in his voice.

These last few months have been marvelous. Being with Hunter has given me a peace I didn't know I could feel. He surprises me with his affection. He treats himself to a coffee from Peet's Coffee and Tea on Fridays after his morning meetings. Once we started dating, he started treating me too. But I'm in class by the time he goes. So, every Friday, he stops in and drops me off a hibiscus tea. He didn't want my principal to get irritated with him, so the first time he did it, he also brought her a coffee. The second time, he brought our secretary a drink. By the third time, he ordered two to-go party sizes, one with coffee and one with tea for all the staff. But he always hand-delivers mine.

I recline my seat a bit and close my eyes, trying to calm my nerves before I finally share my story with him.

"SWEETNESS? Jules? It's time to wake up, sleepyhead."

I feel my leg being shaken. I try to move my head, but my neck screams at me in anger. I rub my neck and look over to Hunter. "What's going on?" I look around, confused.

He throws his head back and laughs. "Just how little sleep did you get last night? When you said you only slept a little, I didn't grasp how serious you were."

I look around and recognize the landmarks around us as the city of Redmond. "Oh my gosh, did I sleep the entire ride?"

I pull the visor down and open the mirror. The dried drool on the right of my mouth is a good sign I slept hard. I wipe under my eyes, trying to remove any makeup that smudged during my unplanned nap. "I can't believe I slept the whole way. I am so sorry, Hunter."

He strokes my thigh and squeezes right above my knee. "Babe, you needed it. Plus, we know you're a horrible road trip partner. You always fall asleep in the car," he teases, but I still feel guilty.

As his phone speaks the next direction prompt, I realize we're about to turn onto my parents' street. I never had a chance to talk to him.

"Hunter, can we drive around a bit more? Or maybe go to the next street and just park?"

But he turns my car into my parents' driveway and puts it into park.

He looks at me, probably assuming my weirdness is all anxiety over him meeting my parents. "Don't worry, Jules. We're okay."

*I'm out of time.*

My parents must have been waiting at the door like little kids waiting for a friend. Because as soon as my car enters their driveway, they have the front door open and are coming out to greet us.

I take a deep breath as I exit the car.

My time is up.

21

JULES

"Jules, Hunter. Welcome. You two made great time," my mom states as she pulls me into an embrace.

Hunter puts his hand out to greet my father. "Hunter Peterson, sir. It's a pleasure to meet you both. And I will say I made good time. That one fell asleep about five minutes into the drive. I had to wake her up when we got off the highway." My dad and Hunter laugh while shaking hands. Then, Hunter moves to introduce himself to my mother.

She slaps his hand away and pulls him into a hug. I can't hear what she whispers to him, but whatever it is puts an even bigger smile on his face and pulls his gaze to me.

"Did no one warn you she can't stay awake in a car? She's been like that since the day we brought her home." My dad laughs. "Even with Mitch screaming in the back next to her, she just slept."

My breath stutters. We've been here two minutes, and they already brought Mitch up. Obviously, my dad did nothing wrong by telling a story about his daughter and son. *Oh God. What are my parents going to think when they find out I haven't told Hunter about Mitch?*

"Hunter, why don't you and Bob grab the bags and we can all head inside? We held dinner, so I hope you two came hungry."

With one of our arms around the other's waist, my mom and I walk toward the front door. I look over my shoulder and see Hunter and my dad talking easily. He fits in with my family. I thought he would. But now that I see it, I know even more than before that I made a mistake holding so much back from him. I just pray things will be okay with us.

"You can just leave the bags by the stairs and take them up later," my mom says. "Forgive me, I know I'm old-fashioned, but I ask that you two don't share a room this weekend. Jules, you will obviously be in your room, and Hunter, you can have the guest room."

I roll my eyes and turn toward her. "Mom, that's a bit extreme, don't you think?"

"My house, my rules." She gives me a stern look.

"Mrs. Morgan, no worries. I'm just happy to be here," Hunter offers.

"I might be old-fashioned, but please, call me Kathleen," she says, and Hunter nods. "Okay, well, take your shoes off and come into the house and get comfortable. Dinner will be ready in five." With that, my mom walks into the kitchen.

I'm hoping I can pull Hunter aside after dinner and explain things to him. But that hope is quickly dashed.

"These photos are great," Hunter muses as he looks at all our family photos hanging in the front room. There are at least thirty frames. Of my grandparents' (on both sides) wedding photos, my parents' wedding, and memories throughout the years of me and Mitch. And then, something that should have never happened—my accomplishments and life moments that surpassed my older brother's.

My eyes quickly dart from the different photos to Hunter's face. I watch him closely, witnessing the very moment in which he gets confused. There are so many photos of me and Mitch together over the years. A handful of photos of the four of us posed together.

Hunter looks at me and says, "Who is this?"

I don't need to look to see who he's pointing to.

Before I can answer, I hear my dad say, "Oh, that's Mitch. Jules, have you never shown Hunter a picture of your brother?" He says it with a laugh, but there is no humor in this moment.

"Brother? You have a brother?"

A plate breaks behind him. The butter and knife that were on it scatter. My mom just stands there gawking at me. All three of them are staring at me. Hunter looks confused. My parents study me with disappointment.

Nothing comes to me. I can't explain this away.

My mom, even when disappointed in me, is still one of my biggest supporters, and she speaks first. "Oh, silly me. Bob, can you get the broom for me?" To me and Hunter, she says, "How about you two go enjoy a moment out back, and we'll holler when we have all of this cleaned up?"

Hunter follows me outside and, to my surprise, he's calm. "Jules, what is going on?"

I put my hand on his chest and try to find his heartbeat to calm my own. "I have no good reason for not telling you sooner. It's actually what I wanted to talk to you about when we got in the car. I had an older brother—Mitch. That's who's in all those photos." I smile, knowing it's a forced expression.

Hunter covers my hand on his chest, just nodding at me for a moment before speaking. "Had?"

I puff out my cheeks and blow out a long breath. "Yes, *had*. He was killed when he was eighteen—a senior in high school— by a drunk driver."

Hunter takes a step back and turns away from me. He runs his fingers through his hair a handful of times.

I'm not sure what he's thinking, so I continue. "I've thought about telling you so many times. I don't know why I didn't. It hurts to talk about him. I'm not trying to make an excuse. But this is hard for me."

Hunter turns around and strokes my cheek with his thumb. "I want you to know I am here for you. I want you to share things with me. I'm not mad. I just wonder why you didn't feel like you could tell me."

I pace. "It wrecked me when it happened. No. That's wrong. It wrecked all of us, for years. I'm sorry I didn't tell you. It's so hard to talk about. It changed the whole trajectory of my life. I just never knew how to bring him up." The tears I've been fighting start to fall down my face.

Hunter walks closer to me and engulfs me. "Shh, it's okay. I was just taken aback, is all. I'm trying to process it all, okay?" He rubs my back with one arm while he tightens his hold on me with the other. "Any other major life moments you need to share with me?"

It's the perfect opening to tell him about Matt. My first love. I swallow and step back before speaking.

"Okay, you two come on in for dinner," my dad interrupts, standing there with the slider open and waiting for us to come in.

I should grab Hunter's arm and stop him from walking in. I should tell my dad to give us a few more minutes.

But I don't.

## 22

# HUNTER

*O*nce Jules and I go inside for dinner, I feel stuck. Her parents still seem a bit sad. I don't know if I should say something to them about Mitch. I should have offered my condolences on their son's passing. But selfishly, I was stuck thinking about what it meant that Jules never shared any of this with me. Hell, what is one supposed to say in this situation?

In a way, I feel like they're judging our relationship because she never told me. In a way, I think I am, too. I heard what she said before dinner. Yet, I still wonder why she never felt comfortable enough with me to share.

Dinner is quiet. Her parents are lovely and make polite conversation, but it feels forced. After dinner, I offer to clear the table. After all, they made us such a lovely meal.

"Hey, you. You okay?" Jules comes up behind me and puts her arms around my waist.

"Yeah, I just have a headache. I think it's from the drive." *But it's probably a tension headache.*

As much as it bothers me how I found out about her brother, I know I'm no better. I haven't been totally honest with her about my own past.

"Okay. Well, my mom was asking if I'd go run some errands with her tomorrow. Would you mind? I promise it won't be for too long. She just wants to get some last-minute things for the party."

"No, that's fine. Do you want me to tag along?"

Just then, their front door opens. We walk into the family room which leads to the front door. Jules moves next to me and laces our fingers together. I look at her, as I can feel her body tense.

"Eric. Perfect timing. We're just about to have dessert, and Hunter was just wondering what he should do tomorrow while Jules and I shop. But first, Jules, how about you make introductions?" Kathleen gets up from the loveseat she was sharing with Bob and heads back into the kitchen, I presume to get dessert.

I look at Jules, our hands still linked.

"Um, Hunter, this is Eric. He's a family friend." She looks to him, then back to me. "Eric, this is my boyfriend, Hunter."

I step toward him but keep my grip on Jules. Yeah, it's pretty much me marking her as mine, but something about the way this guy is looking at her irritates me. Not to mention how comfortable he is with her family that he just walked in. *Who does that?*

"Nice to meet you—Eric, is it?" I say.

The prick doesn't even speak; he just nods his head once with his chin out. He's shorter than me by a couple of inches, but he looks like he's trying to stand taller, and all of a sudden, his chest is out. *Where did this guy come from?*

I squeeze Jules's hand and smile at her. Her smile back makes me feel a bit more relaxed. Her mom comes back in with a tray filled with lemon bars for dessert.

"Oh, Kat, you know I love these. Mind if I take two?"

*Kat?* Before Kathleen responds, Eric grabs two bars and happily chomps on one. Kathleen looks unfazed by his nickname for her, once again making me feel like an outsider in this gathering.

"How are you, Smalls?" he says to Jules.

Now, not only do I feel like an outsider, but I get the feeling this idiot is flirting with my girl right in front of my face. Thankfully, when I look at Jules, she looks just as irritated.

She turns to me and says, "Smalls was my nickname when I was like, nine, and a pest to my brother and his friends because I was the only girl and they had to include me." She gives me a small smile, then turns her attention to Eric. "Please don't call me that. I hate it."

Eric puts his hands up in surrender.

"And I'm good," she adds. "Great, actually." She looks back at me, and I feel like I won whatever pissing match I unknowingly walked into.

I let go of her hand and put my arm around her, pulling her to me and kissing the top of her head.

She snuggles into my chest, then asks him, "What are you doing here, Eric?"

"Jules Eleanor Morgan, *manners*. That's what I was getting around to. While you and I are off shopping tomorrow, Eric here offered to take Hunter out for a beer. Isn't that thoughtful of him?"

Jules pales before my eyes, drawing my attention from her mom to her.

"You okay, babe?" I ask, but she doesn't look at me.

She looks straight ahead, her stare locked onto her mom's. She bounces on the balls of her feet. She is clearly uncomfortable with her mom's idea, but why?

Finally, she says, "Mom, I think Hunter would feel awkward hanging out with someone he doesn't even know. No offense, Eric."

"Aww, I think he can handle it. Can't you, Hunter?" Eric chimes in.

I don't even bother looking at Eric, directing my answer to Jules. "Nah, it's cool. This way, you and your mom get some time together, just the two of you."

Jules turns her attention to me. "I don't think it's a good idea, Hunter. I asked you here to spend time with us, not to pawn you off."

Man, she's nervous about this. *Who is this guy?* My gaze goes from Jules to Eric and back to Jules. *Is he an ex?*

"Jules, sweetie, you're being silly. You act like Eric is some weirdo." Kathleen laughs and puts her hand on Eric's bicep. It's obvious Jules's parents and Eric are very comfortable around one another. "It's very kind of him to do this. And Hunter himself said it's fine. Thanks, Hunter."

Kathleen gathers the dessert plates from both Eric and Bob. Neither Jules nor I ate. Man, I am failing at this meet-the-parents thing.

I grab a lemon bar and take a bite. "Mmm. This is excellent, Kathleen. Thank you for going to so much trouble for our visit. I appreciate it."

She pats my shoulder. Jules stands to go after her mom, but I reach out to her and whisper, "What has you rattled?"

"I'm not rattled. I just think it's rude of my mom to expect you to hang out with some guy you don't know. That's all."

"I didn't know your parents till a few hours ago and I hung out with them." I smile, trying to break some of the tension.

"You did that for me. This is different. It's stupid." She looks from me to Eric, staying on him for a beat too long in my mind.

"I'd still be doing it for you," I tell her.

She steps back from me and smiles. But it doesn't reach her eyes. I can tell this is unnerving her. This entire day is throwing me off.

Eric, thankfully, doesn't stay for long and leaves, saying he'll catch me tomorrow.

Jules and I help her parents clean up. Shortly after, I follow her up the stairs and we kiss goodnight. Then, I retreat to my separate room.

At first, when I heard we'd be in separate rooms, I thought it was stupid. Now, I'm glad for the solitude.

I feel a foreboding that something is coming. Something I can't stop, and something that won't be positive.

23

# JULES

*a*s I sit at my vanity finishing putting my makeup on for the day, my stomach is still in knots from yesterday. Hunter said we were okay last night, but I could tell something was off. Perhaps he's upset with me for not telling him about Mitch sooner. And now, he'll be spending the afternoon with Eric.

*What's Eric's motivation?* I don't trust him. I look at my clock —it's late enough. I reach for my phone.

**Me**: You're taking my boyfriend out for a drink? What is up, Eric?

**Eric**: Boyfriend, huh? Your mom only said a friend of yours. I'm just being the nice guy I am. Chill out, Jules.

**Me**: Please, Eric. I like this guy, okay? Be nice.

**Eric**: I am always nice, Jules. Everyone but you can see all I want is for you to be happy.

**Me**: I am happy. Please let me leave Redmond happy.

After tossing my phone onto my bed, I stare at my pink duvet. I hate pink. I've had this stupid duvet since right after the funerals. I had thirty dollars. I remember driving to the store. At the time, I didn't care what I bought; I just needed new bedding.

I had cried myself to sleep night after night, smelling my old bedding, trying to find Matt. I never did. It wasn't healthy, let alone normal. I'm not sure what my mom thought my sudden bed makeover was about. Thirty dollars bought me new sheets that were scratchy and a clearance Pepto Bismol pink duvet. Why I never bought something else in all these years, I can't answer for the life of me.

I hear the floors creak out in the hallway. *Is Hunter up?* I slowly open the door, and standing before me is the most handsome man. God, he legitimately steals my breath. I always thought that was such a stupid saying, yet somehow, it perfectly describes how I feel every time I see him.

"Morning," I say.

"Morning, beautiful."

My smile is instantaneous. Apparently, that's all the green light he needs because in the next moment, my back hits the wall after he shoves us both into my room. He quietly closes my bedroom door and holds my face, just looking at me.

"Hi, sweetness." He takes a deep breath. "I sure do...I mean, I missed you."

My stomach flips. Why does it feel like—as he's standing there with both hands on my face, looking so deeply at me—he was about to tell me he loves me? I place my hands on his, before touching up his arms and down his sides. I pull him closer to me. Our kiss is frantic. I think we are both on edge, and it feels like we're punishing each other with our mouths. We pull apart when air is necessary.

"I want you so bad," he whispers.

"I'll be quiet. I need you, Hunter. Please."

"Your parents didn't even want us in the same room, and you want me to have sex with you? They're both awake. I could hear them when I was in the hallway. No way. I'm trying to get them to like me, not toss me out."

"They like you. I'm not sure how I feel right now. You really won't touch me?" I step around him.

With our eyes locked, I unbutton my blouse, giving myself a mental fist bump for putting on an alluring bra this morning. It's black lace with pink-and-black straps that crisscross in the back. Why does provocative lingerie make me feel so confident? That look in Hunter's eyes makes me feel powerful. I skim my fingers up and down my exposed skin. My touch is featherlight, but the effect is much ampler.

"Fuck. What are you trying to do to me? I'm trying my hardest to be well-behaved in your parents' home. You are the devil tempting me right now."

His breathing has increased, and as I lower my gaze, I see he's excited with my mini striptease. "Hardest? Pun intended?" I shimmy out of my blouse and saunter over to him, putting a little extra sway in my hips. Splaying my hands against his hard chest, I push until his back hits the wall. "If you won't touch me, I'm going to touch you."

As I lower his zipper, I sink to my knees. I look up at him, unfastening his pants. I lower both his jeans and boxers together. As my lips surround him, his breath hisses.

I lick the underside up to the tip, never taking my gaze off his. When I take him in as far as I can and he's hitting the back of my throat, he closes his eyes, no longer able to keep them open. His one hand goes to the back of my head, gathering as much hair as he can. He tries to control my speed, but I have both hands around his backside, and I keep sucking until there's nothing left.

With Hunter in my room now, I don't think about the weirdness that settled over us before. I don't worry about him going out with Eric. Hunter makes me feel confident, feminine, desired, and in this moment, I feel in control.

I wipe my bottom lip and stand. His breathing is labored. I walk over to my mirror and fix my makeup the best I can and brush out my hair. When I turn back around, Hunter is still against the wall, his pants around his ankles.

"I'm the luckiest son of a bitch," he says.

I smirk at him and blow him a kiss as I pick my clothes up and redress. "I—"

It hits me like a ton of bricks that I almost just said I love him. We haven't uttered those words yet. I don't know if I'm ready to.

I clear my throat and say, "I hope you have at least a little fun today, but consider that my apology for this afternoon." I walk over and give him a quick kiss. I'm so turned on from what I just did, if I give more than a quick peck, we won't be leaving this room.

With that, I walk out and downstairs to leave with my mom.

I TRY to get wrapped up in our errand running so I won't worry about Hunter hanging out with Eric. He's getting picked up at three, and as the clock gets closer to that time, I can feel my unease increase. *What is wrong with me? I mean, what do I think Eric will really do?* Just as I'm mentally calming myself down while my mom drones on about flowers, my stomach clenches at the sound of a voice.

"Wow, if it isn't the prodigal daughter."

I roll my eyes, but only my mother can see it. I haven't seen Hannah much since my brother's funeral. We were never close, so there was no reason to keep up a relationship with her. Sure, she dated him, but I highly doubt their relationship would have lasted past high school regardless of what happened.

My mom giggles and shakes her head at me, chastising me.

I slowly turn to face Hannah. "Hi, Hannah. I haven't seen you in a while. How are you?" I don't care how she is, but with my mom with me, I summon up the bare minimum decorum my parents raised me with.

She looks the same, almost eerily. She has the same hairstyle and clothing choice; even her makeup is the same. *Maybe someone is afraid to move past the glory days of high school?*

"I'm good," she says. "Unlike some, I realized what an amazing life I had here in Redmond and moved back after college. This is my shop. Cute, isn't it? I am so blessed. Hello, Kathleen. Are you here picking out flowers for the big birthday bash?"

"Hello, Hannah dear. Yes, I am. Why I waited so long to do this, I have no idea. There are so many beautiful arrangements in your shop. You are talented."

"Why, thank you. I'm sure if Jules here was around more, you'd have come in sooner. Things like this are always more fun to do together. Gosh, my mom and I get together once a week."

At this point, I'm not even trying to hide my irritation.

My mom, on the other hand, is eating up all the crap Hannah's serving. "Oh, that sounds so lovely. I would love if Jules moved closer. I don't know if that dream is fading or not with this guy she's now seeing."

At the mention of Hunter, my mind flashes to this morning in my room, and I smile my first genuine one since Hannah approached. I feel surer of myself. Hannah always tries to make me feel small.

"That's nice you've finally found someone," she says. "I don't think I've ever heard of you dating anyone. Gosh, not much experience. You better hold on to this one, or who knows when the next guy will come along." She laughs—more like cackles.

I hate her. I've always made impulsive choices when irritated. It's stupid and childish, but it doesn't stop me. "No worries about that. I shouldn't say anything, but we went ring shopping. He didn't want to take anything away from my dad's party, so we're waiting. He's amazing. I'm so *blessed*."

*What the hell? Why did I say that?*

I can feel my mom's stare boring into me. I risk a quick glance, and she's looking at me with her mouth wide open. I think she can see the pleading in my stare, so she tries to recover quickly.

"Oh, yes. Hunter will be such a wonderful addition to our family," my mom says.

After that, we quickly make our selections for the party flowers. I have to get out of here before I've not only made up a fake engagement but also pretend to be pregnant or something. *Dear Lord, I am stupid.* I am well into my twenties, but a few minutes around Hannah and I feel like I'm back in high school.

When we're five feet away from the door closing, walking down the sidewalk to our next stop, my mom regains her speech. "Well, that was an interesting development. Any truth to it?"

"Mom, I would have told you if I were engaged. I know that was a dumb thing to say. But something about her always brings the stupid out of me."

"I have no idea why you two ladies could never get along. Not even for your brother."

The mention of Mitch always changes the mood. Or at least, I feel like it does. "I'm sorry, Mom. I acted like a child in there. I can go back in and correct what I said."

She puts her hand on my arm. "No, that's silly. Who cares what Hannah thinks or says? If I hear rumors about it, I'll just wave them off. It's Redmond. Things always spread so fast around here. Even with the town growing so much in the last decade, it still feels small to me. Probably too small for you, especially after Portland."

The talk of when I'm coming back always happens at some point in a visit home. "Mom, you know I love you and Dad. I love seeing you. But I don't see myself ever moving back, regardless of Hunter. I'm sorry if that hurts you."

"I want *you* happy, baby girl. That's what I want. If that means you're here, wonderful. If it means you're somewhere else, I'll miss you, but as long as you're happy, I'm happy."

"I can honestly say I am happy." I fidget with my bracelet, knowing I need to apologize to her. "Mom, I'm sorry about last night. That I didn't tell Hunter about Mitch."

Sadness cascades over her face. "I wondered about that."

I pull her into a hug. "It's just hard for me. I think of Mitch daily, he's always with me. Heck, I still talk to him when I need him."

A tear falls down her cheek. "So do I." She puts both hands on the sides of my face. "I'm stronger now. We can talk about him. I miss him every day." She stops and closes her eyes for a moment. "We weren't there for you like you deserved when it all happened. I'm sorry for that."

"I know, Mama. I love you so much."

We embrace again and just hold each other for a moment on the middle of the sidewalk.

Then I say, "Okay, now let's tackle that party list. What else do we need to get?"

And just like that, we move along and finish our to-do list.

24

# HUNTER

hy did I agree to grab a drink with some guy I don't know and don't care to know? Who is he to Jules's family again? Her mom's best friend's son? Whatever. I will think of it like any business meeting I go into. It'll be friendly and quick. As long as Jules is happy, I don't care. Actually, she didn't seem too happy about me going out with this guy. I still wonder why.

She was different this morning. It was hot. I've never seen her take control like that. I'm a lucky asshole to have her. Hell, I almost told her I love her. And that was *before* the blowjob. The feelings have been growing for a while now. I thought it was too soon at first. Then I decided it didn't matter. What matters is I want to make her feel cared for and make as many of her dreams come true as I can.

I hear the knock right at three. Punctual guy. Jules's dad had to go run some errands of his own, so he left me a key to lock up.

I open the door, and sunlight pours in. I shield my eyes with my forearm.

Eric greets me, and just like last night, he looks me over and puffs out his chest. I get the feeling this guy sees me as competition, and it makes me wonder, once again, who he is to Jules. She said he's just a family friend. I have no reason to doubt her.

"Hunter."

I put my hand out to shake his, but he just stands there. "Thanks for offering to grab a drink with me. Nice of you."

"To be honest, Kat asked my mom, and my mom asked me. Jules is going to be busy all day with her mom. We didn't want her to feel awkward leaving you."

I laugh. "I don't need a babysitter. If you don't want to do this, I'm just fine staying here. Up to you."

"Nah, everyone's expecting this to happen. One drink won't take long. Let's go." At that, he turns and starts walking.

This guy seems like someone who feels he has a lot to prove. I hate doing business with people like that. Their ego makes decisions for them that most levelheaded people wouldn't make.

The ride to the bar is quick and...in a squad car. "An officer, huh? I didn't realize you guys could drive around like normal in your squad car. To a bar, no less. Kind of odd, don't you think?"

"You never know when it'll come in handy."

Odd response. Again, I feel like this guy wants to intimidate me. All he does is make me feel sorry for him. He seems like he's carrying around a chip.

When we walk into the bar, I can't help but look at my watch. An hour seems courteous. I can be around this guy for an hour.

"Give me a stout. Hunter, what'll you have?"

"I'll take an IPA, thanks."

We sit down with our beers at a high bar table. The place is nice, but not as nice as Portland Social. Even though I had nothing to do with that place other than banking it, I still feel pride. I now compare places to it.

"So, what do you do, Hunter?"

"I run an investment firm in Portland."

"That's what your daddy gave you. I asked what you do."

"I manage other people's money. Sometimes we help invest in new businesses to get them up and running." I tap my finger on the table.

"Sounds boring as fuck." He takes a drink of his beer. "Dating Jules, huh? You're like a unicorn."

I cock my head to the side and look at him for a moment. "How's that?"

"She doesn't date. Like, at all. You're the first guy I've heard of."

"Do you hear from her often?" I casually ask him.

"Jealous, Hunter?" He smirks at me.

I'm not jealous, but I am curious. "No, man. Not one bit. I am aware of what we have. There's no reason to be jealous of the small parts of her others get." It's an asshole comment, but this guy makes me feel like marking Jules as mine.

I take a drink of my beer and notice an attractive brunette walking up behind Eric. She slinks one arm around his neck and stands next to him. She turns her smile on me. My stomach feels uneasy with her here.

"Hello, boys. Playing nicely?" She giggles.

"Hey, Hannah. Shouldn't you be at your shop?" Eric says.

"It's my lunch, and I heard you were showing Jules's new guy around. So I thought I'd pop in to see the guy who's marrying our Jules." She runs her gaze over me like she's picking out a snack.

Eric chokes on his beer, and I know I look shocked. Marrying Jules? What is she talking about? And why does hearing that make me feel happy, like throwing my fist in the air in victory? Shit, I haven't even told her I love her, and now my brain is latching on to the idea of marriage. I need to slow down.

"Hannah, what are you talking about? Stop trying to start shit. Jules isn't marrying this guy."

She puts her hands up like she's about to defend herself

against an assailant. "Sorry, but that's what I heard. From Jules, no less."

Eric turns to look at me so fast I wouldn't be surprised if he pulled a muscle in his neck. I see his clenched jaw. I have no idea what this girl is talking about, but I know it'll be better to just let her talk than ask questions.

"You're engaged? Since when?" Eric is seething now. *Interesting.*

When I stay silent, Hannah answers for me. "Jules said it just happened, but they didn't want to take away from the party so they're waiting to announce it until after. Like anyone would care about her getting engaged. She's so full of herself."

*Jules told her we're engaged?* Well, if that's what she wants people to think, I'm game.

"You're engaged?" Eric asks again.

"Like the amiable lady said, we didn't want it announced. I'm shocked Jules said something, but I'm going to respect what we discussed earlier and just say whatever Jules said is the truth."

"I can't fucking believe this. You? She's going to marry *you*?" Eric says.

"I don't know what your problem is, buddy. But don't worry about finishing this man-date that was set up for us. I'm going to head out. It was fascinating meeting both of you."

Eric stands to block me. "We aren't done. Hannah, go get your food and head out."

She takes one more look at me and smiles, and it somehow makes her look even bitchier. She came in looking to start shit, and she hit her mark.

Eric points his finger at me. "You need to hear some things before you leave."

Curiosity gets the best of me. I should listen to my gut, but I stay. "What do you want, Eric?"

"Do you know who I am?"

"A family friend." I shrug. I have no idea where this is going, but I want him to hurry up. "What is this? Are you stepping in for her brother and trying to give me the are-you-worthy talk?"

"I definitely don't want to be Jules's brother. I gather she told you about Mitch. But what did she tell you about Matt?"

"Who's Matt?" My question looks like it shocks him.

He shakes his head, looking down at the table. I can see heartbreak wash over him. *What the hell is going on?*

"Matt was my brother. He was in the car with Mitch when they got into the accident. I genuinely wish I could say I'm surprised she didn't tell you about him. But fuck, I wish she did. She doesn't think anyone knows. I'm not sure why. They weren't that careful."

"Her brother and yours weren't careful?"

"No, Jules and Matt weren't careful. They were dating when the accident happened. I always wondered if something was going on with them. My brother knew I liked her, so I think he was scared to tell me. It was obvious he was seeing someone. He was so happy it was sickening. Mitch would have been weirded out, though. I assume that's why they didn't tell anyone. To this day, though, she hasn't really talked about Matt. It sucks. But that's the way Jules is. She just shoves it all down and keeps moving. Are you aware of what happened? How they died?"

"Jules said it was a drunk driver."

He shakes his head again. He goes to take another drink, but he already drank it all. "Crap." He looks at the bartender and swings his beer back and forth between his fingers, signaling he wants another. He jerks his chin to me, silently asking if I want another one.

"No thanks."

"Yeah, a drunk driver." He sits there looking me over, dissecting me, and something clicks for me.

"Hey, how did you know I took over my investment firm?"

"You've noticed I'm a cop, right?"

"Yeah, the ride in the squad car on the way here kind of gave it away."

He chuckles. "I ran into Jules's mom right around Christmas. She was excited to share that Jules had met someone. I encouraged her to ask Jules for your full name so she could Google you. I was still with her when Jules texted her back. So, I filed it away. She didn't tell you any of this? We talked all about it when she was home with us for the holiday." He gives a snide grin. "Anyway, when I heard she was bringing you to the party, I admit I looked you up myself." He lifts one side of his mouth up in a smirk. "I know about your parents. About the guy who adopted you. Does Jules?"

I feel like my lungs are in a vise. I can't get a full breath. This ass has dug into my past. My parents' mistakes weren't mine, but I still carry the guilt. I wish now that I had gotten that second beer. *Fuck, that is ironic.*

"She knows about me being adopted, but not why." I don't understand why I'm sharing so much with him, but this conversation feels like a gut-punch.

He nods his head like he gets it. "Kind of weird, don't you think? You guys have been dating for a bit, talking about marriage, and yet the biggest moments in each other's lives, you haven't talked about. Don't you think that's odd?"

I huff out a breath and shoot him a dirty look.

"I'm not some asshole trying to cause trouble. I care about Jules. More than she wants me to, I admit that." Eric tosses some peanuts from the bowl on our table into his mouth. "I don't think you two truly know each other. Jules is important to me and I want the best for her. I don't believe that's you."

"Fuck you." I point my finger at him. "You don't know what you're talking about."

I'm seething now. I need to get out of here. More than a few patrons are looking our way.

Just what I need—to get in a fight with a local who just so happens to be a cop.

I was ten when my life went from bad to worse. My dad was drunk off his ass, *again*. He and my mom were fighting, and he grabbed the keys saying he needed another beer. My mom yelled at him to stay. He refused, so she got in the car with him. Neither one of them thought about me. They never did. They just left. My dad hated me, and my mom's priority was always him.

"I read the files," Eric says. "You had a shit life, Hunter. I can't imagine anyone growing up like that. The girl was seventeen? Young. Just like my brother and Mitch."

I nod, my eyes unfocused as I remember back. The policewoman was so nice. Her voice was so calming. She said there'd been an accident. I was happy when I heard this. That for once, my parents' absence wasn't because of their lack of love.

"Man, I can't even. I'm sorry, Hunter. You were lucky, though. You weren't a ward of the state for long."

"You're an ass." I shake my head, trying to gather control. "What do you want, Eric? Why bring all this up? Do you think you're going to get Jules for yourself by telling her my horrible parents killed an innocent just like her brother? Is that your plan?"

"I don't have a plan. I'm only pointing out the obvious. That you two don't know each other. Question, ever notice she doesn't like to drink?"

"Ha. I've been around her plenty when she's drinking."

Eric smiles like I just stepped into his trap. "White wine, right?" He smirks when he can read the answer on my face. "Yeah, white is her go-to. Usually, she puts it down, or *forgets it* somewhere, or will say she finished it already. Sometimes she will take sips. But she doesn't like feeling out of control, so she usually won't drink at all. But if she is comfortable, she's a whiskey girl. Ever have a whiskey with her, Hunter? In fact,

Jules and I shared some Green Spot when she was home for Christmas."

I think back to all the times we've been together and she had a drink. *Have I ever actually seen her drink?* And whiskey? I've never seen her drink whiskey. This ass could be lying, but I feel like he isn't. "Shit."

"Don't beat yourself up for not noticing. I've known her since we were kids, and it took me a while. As I said, I don't think you really know her. Last question. Do you honestly think she won't care about your parents, what they did? That it won't taint the way she sees you? Can you guarantee it?"

I hate this guy. He's messing with my head—trying to get under my skin and make me question what Jules and I have. *We're solid, aren't we? Why haven't we talked about any of this yet?* We haven't been seeing each other all that long. That's probably why. But that excuse just doesn't sit right with me.

"You're obviously going to do what you want. But I want you to know, if you don't tell Jules about your parents, I will. You two seem to have a hard time sharing with each other. She deserves to know. She deserves the right person."

I laugh at that. *Selfish prick.* He has his own agenda. "Right. Let me guess, that person is you? You want me out of the picture and Jules back here in Redmond."

"Nah. Jules has made it extremely clear there is no *us*. But her plan was always to come back. After all they lost, Jules and her parents need one another. But she won't leave Portland because of you. Some guy she doesn't even genuinely know. Seems like a regret destined to happen, don't you think?"

I have to get away from this guy. I toss a twenty on the table and start to walk away, but then I walk back to him. "I don't know what today was for you. I would have given her the world. All you did today was destroy a chance at happiness for her. You could have gone about this so many ways that would have painted you favorably. But I can guarantee you will be nothing but the villain in her story."

With that, I walk out of the bar. I have no idea where the hell I am or where to go in this town, but I need air and I can't get any around that guy. *How did all of this get so messed up?*

It's after six by the time I make it back to Jules's parents' house. It's warm for this time of year, so her parents have some of their windows open. I can hear her parents' voices coming from inside the house as I walk to the door.

"Did you ask her again about moving back?" I hear Bob ask Jules's mom.

"Yes, Bob. You knew I would. I'd love for her to be back here. But she likes him and won't move back. I think we have to come to terms with that. No matter how much we wish she'd come back like she said she would..."

"Fuck," I swear under my breath. Eavesdropping on her parents is a horrible idea. *What am I doing? What is she doing?* I work up enough courage to open the door.

"Hunter, we were wondering when you'd show. I hope you had a nice time with Eric. He's such a nice guy, isn't he?" Kathleen looks over at me with kindness in her eyes.

Her parents have been so welcoming to me. It makes all of this worse.

"He is something," I offer. "Where's Jules?"

"Upstairs," Kathleen answers, before going to finish what she was doing.

I don't know what I'm going to say, but something needs to happen—and it needs to happen now.

# 25

# JULES

*I* did a thing. After finishing errands with my mom, I was walking downtown, window shopping, and saw the most beautiful bedding set. I love it so much I bought two—one for my place in Portland, and one for here so I have a little piece of home when I visit. Because this place, while I love it and will always have such wonderful memories here, is no longer my home. And I am good with that.

I have my music up as I move my hands across the teal bedding, smoothing out all the wrinkles. I feel so alive as my hips move to the music, but as I turn, I yelp. I didn't hear the door open, so I have no idea how long Hunter's been standing there.

"You scared me. Oh Lord, my heart. I didn't hear you. How long have you been watching?" I walk over to him, smiling. "I missed you. Did you have fun?" I wrap my arms around his neck.

Instead of taking my lips with his in one of our epic kisses, he stands there with his hands loosely resting on my lower back, looking at me. I wait for his response, but it doesn't come.

I drop my right hand and poke him in the ribs, laughing. "Hey, you. What's up? Did something happen?"

"You could say that." He grasps my wrist and removes it from around his neck. He paces, rubbing the back of his neck.

I'm not sure what's going on, but suddenly, I feel chilly. My earlier euphoria is gone.

"Did you tell people we were getting married?" he asks.

"Oh, shit." I run my hand through my loose waves as I blow out a nervous laugh. "Where did you hear that?"

"Someone at the bar said she heard congratulations were in order."

*Hannah.* I knew I shouldn't have said that to her. "What were you doing with Hannah?" Even I can hear the accusatory sound in my voice.

His eyes bulge as he takes me in. "Seriously, Jules? Somehow this is going to be on *me*? I did nothing wrong. I went out with your weird something-to-prove family friend." He puts air quotes around *family friend* for some reason. "He took me to some bar. She showed up. End of story."

His vigorous pacing is not only making my stomach uneasy but my head too; it starts to spin. "So, really, it's a funny story…"

He stops, turns to me, and puts his hand up, effectively stopping me. "Maybe I gave you the wrong impression by coming down here with you. Have I led you on? Given the impression that I'm looking for a wife?"

He hasn't, and I don't want to be marrying someone I've only known for less than a year. But still, his blatant disgust at the thought of it all hurts.

"Whoa, whoa, whoa. What is happening?" I shake my head like doing so might help clear up the fog overtaking me. "I think we need to take a couple of steps back. Let's calm down. What's going on, Hunter? This is us." I reach out to take his hand, but he backs up again.

"I thought we were coming down here for a fun weekend away, and suddenly you are marrying us, and what? Moving back here?"

I step back like he's slapped me. I don't understand the anger. "I said nothing about moving here."

"So, you said we were getting married?"

"This is stupid. Seriously." I laugh, hoping to lighten the mood in my childhood bedroom. "You're making a big deal out of a passing comment."

He starts to speak, so I rush to finish.

"I admit I shouldn't have said it," I tell him. "I said it to someone I went to high school with. Don't you have people from high school that always make you feel small?" Sitting back on my bed, I put my face in my hands, trying to calm myself. "It's stupid, I know, but it just came out. I meant nothing by it. It just happened."

"And moving back?"

"What about it?" I lift my hands, palms up, in a so-what motion. This is a non-topic for me but seems to be the topic du jour for all of the people in my life.

"Do you want to move back here?" he asks.

"Ugh, what is with that question tonight?" I bite my nail. I hate biting my nails. It's an awful habit, and I think it shows insecurity.

"Jules, that isn't an answer. Do you plan to move back here?"

"Where is this coming from?"

"Man, you are dodging this. Funny, today is the first time I heard about it, and it wasn't even from you."

"Please don't tell me what I want for my life."

"What? All I know is I've asked a simple question, multiple times, and you won't answer it. Which is it, Jules—won't or can't?"

"Hold on. I'm just trying to catch up. Yeah, I guess the plan was always to come back here and teach, but—"

"With Matt?"

If I felt slapped before, now I feel as if I've been clubbed. Like one of those fish that won't stop moving so they get hit over the head. Stunned. Just hearing him say Matt's name causes all breath to leave me. I see him taking in my reaction like it's some kind of test.

"*What?* Who? Eric—what did he say? Is this why you're acting all weird? What did he tell you?" I sound crazed, shrill.

"More than you have." He says it so calmly I feel like shoving him to rile him up too.

That's all he says. He drops his little truth bomb and stands there victorious, looking at me like he's won this fight, and what? It's over now?

"You're right. I haven't told you everything. I don't know if that was even a possibility in the short time we've been together." I'm getting over the shock, and now, I'm getting mad. I try taking a few deep breaths because I don't make smart choices when I'm angry or feeling pushed.

"I'm not asking for a full blown briefing on who you are. All I ever wanted was a chance. But you never gave that to me. Not a real one," he says.

"A chance at what? We've been dating. I have given you a chance. You're throwing it all away now, for what?"

"Nah. I never got the chance I wanted. I wanted you to give me the chance to love you. I wanted a chance to show you how astonishing this could be between us. I wanted the chance to take care of you. I wanted a chance for you to maybe fall in love with me. A chance for us to build on what we have. But you never gave me any of that. You don't let anyone in."

I am reeling. He isn't wrong. Maybe I have kept myself walled off. But I legitimately thought I was letting him in. I was trying. I thought he could see that. But no. He doesn't see any part of what I've done—or that all of it is due to my feelings for him.

"Hunter, I've been trying to let you in. I thought I was. I can do better." My voice cracks, and I hate how desperate I sound. "I know I should have told you sooner about Mitch. I should have been more open and shared about Matt."

"This—with us—shouldn't take so much effort. We shouldn't have to keep trying so hard. I get that relationships are work. That you need to wake up every day and choose to fight for that person. But I am tired of fighting for someone who doesn't want to be fought for."

"What are you saying?"

God, how has this day been such a roller coaster? I was on such a high before he came into the room. I realized today that I am *in love* with him. I wanted to share that with him, but not like this. He's so angry with me.

"Answer my question, please. Jules, do you want to move back home?"

"Are we back to this? No, I don't."

"Because of me?"

"I don't know. Sure. Partially, I guess. Because of us. Because Portland feels like home now."

"What if there wasn't?"

I look at him with my brow furrowed, confused by what he's trying to say. "Wasn't what, Hunter?"

"An *us*. If there was no us, you'd be sticking to your plan, right? Because, I'm just saying, I don't think there is enough of an *us* for you to deviate from that plan."

"Not enough of an *us*? What is that supposed to mean? Where is all of this coming from? It can't all be from some stupid comment that Hannah made. She hasn't been a part of my life since high school." I feel sick to my stomach. I don't know where all of this is coming from or where he is trying to go with it all.

I take a deep breath to try to soothe my nerves. I rub small circles over my stomach, trying to calm it. "Hunter, come on.

Where is this coming from? This morning, you were happy. *We were happy. I am sure of that.* I'm happy—well, I was happy, until about ten minutes ago. Please don't make an issue where there is none. Listen to me. Listen to what I want."

"Do you drink?"

"Do I...what?" *Confused. He is confusing me. That question is so out of left field. I think he's making me sick with all of his jumping around. What started all of this again?*

"It's a simple question, Jules. If I handed you an alcoholic beverage right now, would you drink it?"

"I don't know." *There's no point in lying. Either he thinks he knows something, or someone said something.* "No, probably not. I don't really drink. Why? Is that an issue?"

"I don't care if you drink or not. I care that things keep popping up, clueing me in to the fact that I don't really know you."

"I wasn't trying to lie to you. I just...I don't know. How does that come up in a conversation? That first night we met, was I supposed to introduce myself and slip in the fact that drinking makes me feel like I lose control so I don't enjoy it?" *Tears are falling freely down my face. I don't even try to stop them.*

Foolishly, I beg. "Please, Hunter. Let's calm down. I don't want to talk when things are so heated. I don't want us to make a mistake."

"The issue is you've never felt comfortable around me. Not enough to let your guard down. Not enough to share your life with. I kept pushing, thinking it was what you needed. I asked you to let me in, and you never did. I see that clearly now." He runs his hands through his hair, pulling on the strands. "I told you how important honesty is to me. And right now—right now, I feel like I don't legitimately know you. I didn't sign up to be someone's reason to change their life. Don't put that on me."

*I walk over to him. I just need to touch him. If I can touch him and look into his eyes, I can fix this. But damn, that hurt.*

He doesn't want to be my *reason*. I'm not putting anything on him.

"Someone's reason?" I repeat. "Are you kidding me right now? What are you doing? This is us, Hunter. This is me. You know me."

"Do I? I mean, honestly, do I?"

"Wow. I guess I don't actually know *you*."

"What is that supposed to mean? I haven't lied to you," he argues.

"You're right. That I know of, you haven't lied. But I will not stand here and try to convince you I'm worth it. That we are worth it. You don't think what we have is worth it? What was this? Some sort of test I failed? We came all the way here for you to meet my family, and you realized, what? What exactly was I to you? What were we lacking, in your opinion?"

"Jules, don't. I came here because I wanted to. There was no test."

I think I'm going to be sick. I often burp before I throw up, and I just burped three times in a row. I physically can't handle this.

So, I walk over to him and place one hand on his chest, over his heart, and look up into his eyes. I can't read him, though. I have always been able to read him. I'm just standing here like an idiot, looking into his eyes, pleading with mine for him to love me. But it feels like he's already left.

"Are you being serious right now, Hunter? Is this truly how you feel?"

"Yes."

One word seals it. I want to make my hand into a fist and hit him. But that won't change anything. So, I push away from him and steady myself. Even if I don't feel strong, I will try to look like I do.

I wipe the tears that have fallen. "Leave then. But before you go, just realize what you had. You will *never* find anything better."

"Jules, what we had—"

I don't let him finish. "Oh, no." I hold my hand up and point at him. "I didn't say what we had, I said what *you* had. I know what I had. I appreciated you. You made me fall in love with you. But I deserve better than this, so I'm confident I'll find better."

He cracks a bit and starts walking toward me, but stops himself. His hands are in fists at his sides, like it's taking all his restraint not to hold me.

"You're an idiot and I want you to get out." I point at my door. "Now."

Hunter stands there for a moment and opens his mouth.

I foolishly think maybe this will be okay. But when he says nothing, my hopes crash.

He rubs the back of his neck again, then walks out of my room and turns toward our guest room.

A few minutes later, I hear the sound of our front door closing.

I get up to look out of my window that faces the front of the house. I can see the ride-share car out front and wonder when he ordered it. It doesn't matter.

We were never okay.

26

JULES

*I* hid from the world until I couldn't anymore. If I could have skipped my dad's party, I would have. But I'm not that selfish. My dad's party went perfectly—I think.

As I sit here now, I can't remember anything from it, other than my mom's concern. She kept asking if I was okay. We haven't talked about what happened. I guess Hunter texted her to make sure I didn't drive after he left. He didn't want anything to happen to me. She said he texted when he got back to Portland because she asked him to when he was saying his goodbyes to her and my dad. Other than that, I haven't heard from him.

I'm tired of crying. As soon as the party was over, I changed into more comfortable clothes. I hopped in my car, and now, I'm standing in the ice cream aisle at the grocery store. Some ice cream therapy sounds just like what I need.

I'm almost to the end of the aisle with a pint in hand when I hear my name being called. I don't know who I expect to see, but it isn't who stands before me now.

"Mrs. Gregory." I stutter her name. I haven't seen Paula in so long. I can instantly hear her wails the night Matt died. "It's so nice to see you."

We hug briefly, and I tense in her arms. I always feel so much guilt when I see her.

She stares up at me with so much kindness it makes me uncomfortable. "Jules, dear, is everything okay?"

*Okay? No. Your son said something to my boyfriend, and we ended up breaking up. My heart is broken once again. But this time is almost worse. So much worse, because he is still out there in this world, only he doesn't want me.*

*Oh, and by the way, the first time my heart broke, it was by your oldest, but I never told you because I am a guilty, selfish jerk.*

But I can't say all of that to her. "I'll be fine, Mrs. Gregory. Thank you. Nothing some ice cream won't fix."

"Ah, a broken heart." She smiles at me. "I'm sorry, dear. Your mom said you had met someone. She's been excited to meet him. I'm glad I ran into you tonight. I couldn't go to your dad's party. Big groups and I don't get along well anymore. I wanted to call you so many times, but I never knew how to start this."

"Start? Start what?" My heart beats faster. I don't know where the heck this is going, but something tells me I need to prepare.

I watch her chest rise from the deep breath she takes, her gaze jumping back and forth to mine. "I've been wanting to tell you that I know, dear. And I just wanted to say how happy it makes me. More so, I want to thank you." She takes my hands in hers and squeezes them.

I have no clue what she's getting at. My confusion must be clear on my face, for she looks at me with so much sympathy and then closes her eyes.

We stand there for what feels like an eternity. I have no clue what she is talking about. *Should I say something?* I feel like I should, but I don't know. Before I can decide, she clears her throat.

"I remember every word." With her eyelids still closed and her voice quiet but sure, she recites verbatim the last text Matt sent me. "I am so damn sorry. I wanted to tell you, but I chickened out. I was looking right at you, and I fucking chickened out. I love you. I probably just made a bigger mistake telling you for the first time in a text. Shit. But I love you, Jules. You make me so damn happy. I asked your brother if I can eat at your house tonight instead of going home as planned. I just need to see you. I want to say all of this to your beautiful face. But I am texting it to you first so I can't chicken out again. It makes sense to me. I'll see you soon." She opens her eyes, tears coming down both cheeks.

The dam breaks. I couldn't hold back my tears even if I tried. My body ratchets with such force that I'm shaking. I drop my ice cream, and as it rolls away, I search for something to grab ahold of. "How?" I stammer out. "I don't—I don't understand. How?"

She wipes the tears from her face and looks at me with such warmth. "We got ahold of Matt's texts." She walks over and puts a hand over mine. "It always bothered me why he didn't come straight home from practice that night. That had been the plan. I was so angry afterward. Why didn't he stick to the plan? If he had come home, he'd be okay. Why?"

I visibly shake. The years of guilt I've hidden away...

*I am the reason.* I am why her son is no longer walking this planet.

She pauses before continuing. "Then Eric joined the police academy. Once he had a job, he used his connections to get Matt's cell unlocked. We had it from the accident but didn't know his code. We saw his last calls and texts. The last text my boy sent...was to you."

"I am so sorry," I sputter out. I try to dry my face and look her in the eye. I finally ask the one question I've always wondered if people had known the truth about us. "Do you hate me?"

"Oh, honey, how could I ever hate you? Why would you think that?" She strokes my hair.

"Because it's my fault. If it weren't for me, he'd be alive. He changed his plans because of me."

She grabs my face. "I memorized it. I memorized the entire text he sent. It is ingrained in every part of me. Don't you see? He was *happy*, Jules. He was happy when he died. He died right away. He had no clue what happened to him. It happened so fast." She starts to cry. "I am so thankful for that. My baby was lucky. He was happy because of you."

She hugs me tightly and whispers, "That is what I think of. I think of how you made my son absolutely happy, and I am so grateful for that."

She pulls back and looks at me. "My son was the happiest I had ever seen him. That was because of you. I knew he was seeing someone. I just didn't know who. Why didn't you two tell any of us? Not even your mom?"

"At first, we didn't really know what was going on between us. We felt we should tell Mitch first." I shrug. "And after everything, I didn't want to share that part of him with others. I also didn't want people to hate me."

"You have carried around useless guilt. You need to let that go. He didn't die because you loved him. He was living because you did. We don't blame you for anything. I told your mom." She sees my panic right away. "Calm down. I asked her to let me be the one to talk with you first. I'm sorry it's taken me as long as it has."

She holds my hands, rubbing the back of them with her thumbs. "He was a special young man. I'm sure you both loved each other greatly. It made me sad thinking he never got to experience young love. I am so happy to know I was wrong."

We talk for a bit more before I leave, sans ice cream.

BY THE TIME I make it back home, I have replayed that entire scene several times. Something I have been so scared to confront wasn't so scary. I quietly enter my parents' home. However, my discretion isn't needed. My mom is still up, I assume, waiting for me.

"Did she call and tell you?"

"Come here, sweetie." My mom stands with her arms open wide.

Being engulfed in her hugs always makes me feel so small and protected, even though I'm taller than her now. "I'm sorry, Mom."

"Sweetie, you have nothing to apologize for. It makes a few things click for me. I do wish you had told us, but everyone was such a mess back then. No one can fault any of us for how we reacted."

"Thanks, Mom."

"Have you thought about what you're going to do? Are you still leaving tomorrow? What about you and Hunter?"

"I don't know. To any of it."

She twirls my hair like she used to when I was little. "I just want you to remember to open that heart. You've had it walled off for so long. My favorite thing about Hunter was that he got over those walls."

"Yeah, he got over them and then he ran from me," I choke. "Mom, it hurts so much. I...I don't know what to do."

"They say to love deeply and hold on loosely. I think that is said so it doesn't hurt so much when the person leaves. However, I also think you need to hold on loosely because you need to let people go sometimes. Whether that is to literally walk out the door or you need to let them grow and change. You haven't been yourself in a really long time. That's been hard to watch. As your parent, and someone who loves you deeply, I needed to let you figure it out."

"He didn't want me. I don't know what to do with that."

"Jules, he wants you. That man is in love with you. It's obvious. Even your father, who doesn't pick up on anything, said it. I don't know what spooked Hunter. Or where his mind's at. But I can tell you he loves you. Don't...don't do that to yourself. It does no good to try to figure out someone else's motives. Only time will tell what's going to happen between the two of you, but I think you're learning right now that you have some growing to do yourself."

"I've been so scared to move, Mom—in any sense. I somehow convinced myself to stand still. Like if I changed anything, I'd risk everything."

"That's no way to live. Jules, that is no way to *love*. Life is shit sometimes. It just is. Bad things happen with no reason for them. You can't control life so much you neglect living it. I think you try to control so much that you feel you're helping the bad from happening. All you end up doing is stopping all the good. But I think when you took the leap and moved to Portland, that was a positive start. You need to keep the forward momentum, though."

As we hug, she lets me cry.

I don't know what I'm going to do about Hunter. Or if there is anything I can do.

I think my mom is right, though. Before I worry about anyone else, I need to figure myself out.

## 27

## JULES

*A*fter another restless night of sleep and saying goodbye to my parents, I head out of town. But as I pass Redmond's local brewhouse and restaurant, I see a squad car in the parking lot, hoping it's Eric's.

Before I can talk myself out of it, I pull into the parking lot and head inside. I spot Eric right away and walk straight to his table. He's sitting with people I don't know.

"Eric, can we talk?"

"Hey, Jules." He looks me up and down and pops a tater tot into his mouth. "Let's not be rude to my company here. What can I do for you?"

He's coming across so calm, but I can tell he's nervous about what I might say—what I might do.

"Hello, all. Please excuse my interruption. Eric, may I please speak with you outside?" I turn and walk out without waiting for his reply.

He follows me out. "Jules, you can't do that. You can't come in bossing me around."

I step into his space. I'm so mad. "Don't you dare tell me what I can and cannot do. I'm trying to stay calm. But, really?

What the hell were you trying to do?" I see his reply before it even leaves him as he moves his shoulders up like he's about to shrug. "Don't try to tell me you have no idea what I'm talking about."

"I don't like him. There are things you don't know. He's trying to hide things from you, and you deserve to know. You deserve a better man."

"Who? You?" I laugh.

"Why is that such a ridiculous thought? Yeah, me. I'm tired of us tiptoeing around it. We'd be good together. I'd give you a comfortable life. Our families would be so happy." He steps closer, reaching for my hand.

"Eric, there will never be anything between us other than friendship. I appreciate you looking out for me, but no one asked you to."

"Mitch would want me looking after you." He stares at me. "Matt would want me there for you." He holds up a hand once I'm about to argue with him. "Maybe not in the way I want, but he'd want me to make sure you're making the right choices. My brother got to be with you. Why not me?"

For the first time in my life, I slap someone across the face.

*Shit, that hurt.* But my anger outweighs my pain. The sound ricochets off the brick behind Eric, resonating more like a stack of books hitting hardwood. "You're lucky a slap is all you got. Don't talk to me like that again. Don't you talk about what your brother would want, then throw that filth at me in the same breath. I loved him."

My strength is fraying as my voice cracks. "They are *my* choices, Eric. Mine. I might make the wrong ones, but that's my right. Because this is *my* life. I have appreciated your friendship, but that is all we'll ever have between us. And, as of this moment, I don't know if we even have that. I loved your brother. Don't make me hate you."

I take in another breath. This is the first time I've ever said I was in love with Matt to someone else. My eyes close as I do an internal check-in, telling myself it hasn't destroyed me.

I open my eyes. Eric is in uniform, and if one wasn't acquainted with him, they might find him intimidating. He doesn't scare me.

I try to speak more calmly. "I believe you felt you were doing what was best. As am I. You didn't have a right, Eric. But if I hadn't hidden so much, it wouldn't have been as big of a deal." I give a small smile because it's all I can muster.

Then, I turn to leave.

He grabs my forearm, but I refuse to turn around. "I love you, Jules. Maybe not like my brother loved you, but you've been what I've wanted since I was a kid. Long before Matt came around to you. Do you have any idea how that messed with me? That my brother got the girl I wanted."

I finally pivot to look at him, to make sure he hears me. "I was never yours, Eric. We did nothing to hurt you. It just happened. No matter what, he will always be my first love. No one can take that away from me. But it's time for all of us to move on."

"There are things about Hunter you deserve to know."

I shake myself from his grasp and hold up my hands, shaking my head. "Maybe so, but they won't come from you. If I want to know Hunter's secrets, I will ask him for them. I'm mad at you right now. I might be for a while. But all of this didn't come about because of you. I played a part. But, don't call for a while. If I want you to continue to be in my life, I'll reach out to you. Right now, though…I want nothing to do with you."

I turn to leave. There's more he wants to say, but I just can't hear it.

As I head out of Redmond, I see Jericho Lane and take a last-minute detour.

Both my parents and Matt's parents decided on cremation. I don't know if it's a positive or negative, but with cremation, there's no specific place to visit when searching for the one you've lost.

As I pull up to Haystack Reservoir, it's the first time I can say I've felt Matt with me. I've dragged my brother with me wherever I go. He's usually who I turn to when I need to talk something out. He was the person I turned to in life, too. Talking to your deceased brother is better than talking to yourself.

But Matt, I've avoided—the hurt and guilt too vast to face.

This place is where we started, though. One day, as school was ending, Matt saw me in the hallway and asked if I had anything going on. When I told him I was free, he asked if I'd take a drive with him. I had the biggest crush on him, and the thought of being alone in a car with him thrilled and terrified me. But I said yes, and he drove me here, to this reservoir. On the way, we talked about football and school and where he was going to apply for college. But the instant he killed the engine, I felt the air change.

That day, he confessed how he felt about me and asked what my feelings were.

No one was around; just us, the water, God, and Mt. Jefferson. I told him I liked him too, and he gave me the sweetest kiss. It was my first kiss. I don't count Nathan Cox in elementary school. That kiss was like the kind you give your grandma. No, my first kiss was with Matt, and it was gentle and lingered on my lips and mind long after it finished.

Now, as I exit my car and walk a bit—with the sun setting, the water and mountain in view—I check to make sure no one is around. And I do what I haven't done in seven years: I forgive myself.

"Hey, Matt. I'm so sorry it's taken me so long. I actually haven't been here since the last time I came with you. I've really made a mess of things. I don't let myself think of what could have been with us. It hurts too much. But I can't control my dreams. That is when you come to me."

My discipline slips, and my tears fall. "But as of late, you've come less. I don't know what that means. I believe it has something to do with falling for Hunter. He's a good man, Matt. I haven't been very fair to him. It may be too late for me and him. I always seem to be too late in expressing my feelings. I loved you so very much. I'm sorry you never got to hear that. I hope—"

I hiccup from the flow of tears. "I hope you felt it."

I look around at the darkening sky and realize I need to get on the road if I want to make it home by nine tonight. The snow on the peak of the mountain looks lustrous.

I take a deep breath in, feeling a bit lighter. "Thank you for loving me. You taught me how I should be treated. I promise you I'll stop wasting the time I have, and that I'll always carry you in my soul."

I walk back to my car, breathing a little easier. This mini break was far different from what I'd planned for. I can't wish it played out any other way, because it's healed some of the broken fragments inside.

My entire ride home, I keep thinking Hunter should be with me.

As I get off the exit downtown, minutes away from my place, I think about just driving over to Hunter's. I'd make him listen to me.

But then I think of what my mom said. I need to work on myself first.

# HUNTER

*I* open the doors to Portland Social. The place looks pretty busy. I look around, hoping. Though I know she isn't here.

She's probably back from her parents by now. I hope she had fun at her father's party. Her mother was kind when we spoke on the phone—kinder than I deserved. I broke her daughter's heart. Hell, I broke my own heart. I didn't think I could hurt this much without a beating being attached to the pain.

I see Chase busy with a party at the end of the bar. I deflate, wishing for time with my friend.

Then I spot Aiden and stride over to him. "Are you always here? As an investor, I love your enthusiasm for the place. As a human, I have to ask...are you okay, man?"

"Ah, first I was your...what was it?" he says.

"Bar Yoda."

"Ha, yeah. Your bar Yoda. Now I'm what? Jabba the Hutt? Just taking up space?"

I look at him in his jeans, T-shirt, and baseball hat worn low, which seems to be his uniform. He doesn't make much eye contact with me. "Nah, man. You're still my Yoda. It's probably why I came and sat down next to you."

Still staring straight ahead, he tips his beer back. As he puts it back down, he rubs his chin with his index finger, looking like he's pondering the great mysteries of life.

My fingertips stroke the ice inlay in the bar, which keeps the drinks cold. I try chipping away at the ice with my nail.

"Look, man, I'm no one's Yoda. Trust me. Anyone can give decent advice every now and then, but it's more about the timing of the listener than the giver of advice." He takes another sip. "And yeah, I am here a lot. However, I don't have a drinking problem. I do have plenty of issues, but drinking too much isn't one of them. I just like this place, and Chase lets me be. Simple as that."

"Something tells me you're far from simple. But I'll let it be." I can feel him look over at me, but I do my best to ignore it. After ordering an old-fashioned, I look up at the TV to watch the highlights from the earlier basketball game.

"So, which is it, a new girl with a fresh problem? Or is it the same girl with a different issue?" he asks.

I look down at my just-served drink, playing with the orange peel and muddling it a bit. "Same girl, seemingly the same issue. Add in my own issues, and you have the story."

"Hunter, right?" he checks, and I nod. "Hunter, this girl has brought you in here twice now looking for clarity. You will never find clarity at the bottom of a glass."

"Stop telling my customers not to drink, dick, or I'll stop letting you rest here as much as you do," Chase says, glaring at Aiden, but then he welcomes me with a smile. "Already fuck things up there, Prince Charming? I got a slew of angry texts from her roommate."

"Why the hell is Gretchen texting you about me?"

"I think she was hoping I knew what happened, seeing as the ladies don't have a clue. I told her I had no idea about anything that may have happened. Last I heard, you were leaving town to meet the parents. I told her she needed to stay out of it and let you two figure your own stuff out."

"I appreciate that," I tell him.

"So, what happened?" Chase asks.

I choke on my drink. Coughing, I hit my chest a couple of times, trying to calm down. "What about staying out of things and letting us figure out our own stuff?"

"Yeah, that was before you dragged your sorry-looking ass into my bar like a heartbroken puppy. Spill."

"My past caught up to me," I admit, considering Chase had been encouraging me to open up to Jules about my parents. "Plus, it turns out the woman I was falling for keeps even more than I thought locked away inside. I don't know the person I've been sleeping with nearly as well as I thought. Take your pick." I shake my glass, watching the ice move around. I put it back down and glance at the TV, hoping to avoid any more talk about feelings, but it's a commercial break.

Chase just looks at me expectantly, waiting for more information, so I continue.

"It turns out she had a brother, *and* a boyfriend, killed by a drunk driver. All her walls make more sense now. But it doesn't change her not telling me. You can't call that a relationship. It's like she presented me with the social media version of herself. But once you get close, nothing is as it seems."

"Sounds like a lot, man. And similar to what you did. You really think you don't know her?" Chase studies me.

"Honestly? In some ways, I think I know her better than she knows herself. The ride home gave me a lot of time to think about it. I think we are a lot alike, and maybe that's why I felt such a pull to her. Unfortunately, I said a lot of shit I didn't mean. Ultimately, I messed up by leaving. I think that sealed my fate more than anything else, actually."

"Why did you run?"

"A friend of hers looked me up," I admit, and Chase's eyes go wide. "Yeah, the asshole did a full background check. He's a cop. He dug up all about my parents and the accident. He said if I didn't tell her, he was going to. So, like an idiot, I reacted instead of thinking things through. But it all feels too late now. Too much was said." I look away from him. "I can tell you want to say something. Just get on with it and say it." I keep my head down, preparing for something I'm sure I won't like.

Chase knows what bringing my parents up does to my mind. "You overreacted, Hunter. The guy seems like an ass and butted in where he didn't belong. Why let someone like that take power over you?"

He drops his voice, taking a kinder tone. "I get that, to you, your past seems bad, but I don't think you're giving Jules enough credit. Your parents were shit, but you aren't them. You had nothing to do with that accident. It's an unbelievable coincidence that a drunk driver killed her brother and boyfriend. But it wasn't your dad behind the wheel, Hunter. And it sure as hell wasn't you. You need to stop making yourself pay for your parents' mistakes." Chase looks at me, then turns and grabs a rag and starts cleaning.

"She said she loved me, or that I made her fall in love with me. I don't know. Something along those lines." I lean forward in my seat.

Above everything else she said, that's messing with me the most. No one—not my parents, not anyone I've ever dated—has said that to me. I don't even know what to do with it. I don't deserve it right now.

"You okay after hearing that?"

"No. And all that shit you spewed doesn't help my mind right now, either." I pound on the bar twice and blow out a harsh breath. "It sucks hearing it for the only time said like that. I think I love her, but how the hell am I supposed to know?"

Chase leans back against the counter and tosses the towel

over his shoulder. "If you want what's best for her more than you want what you want, then you love her. If being with her makes you feel like a fucking king, then you love her. If you feel a fraction of the way you look, man, you *are* in love."

My fingertips go white. My grip on the glass is so tight, I'm shocked it hasn't shattered. My mind is such a mess right now. I miss Benjamin more today than I have since he passed.

From the moment he moved me into his house, he was always someone I could turn to for solid advice. His advice was always fair, and his demeanor was always calm. He respected me. He never said he loved me, and truthfully, I don't know what it means to be loved. But we respected each other, and that was more than I ever had.

That last time my parents left me alone, I waited for them to come back home. It felt like forever. Eventually, an officer showed up at our door. My father crashed their car—not his first accident, mind you. But it was the first time he hit someone else. My parents were arguing, and my dad crossed into oncoming traffic. The girl didn't have enough time to react. She was seventeen. They all died at the scene.

After two months in foster care, I was finally placed. That is how I came to live with Benjamin.

Benjamin and I were never extremely close. Don't get me wrong, he was always kind to me. I have nothing but respect for the man. But there was no love in the house. I think that's why I responded how I had to Jules. I didn't understand the feeling I was experiencing, and I took it out on her, unfortunately.

I've never shared about my past with anyone but Chase. I felt strongly when I learned how much Jules kept from me, but I'd done no better.

I hear someone clearing their throat, bringing me out of my thoughts. I pick my head up and turn toward Aiden. "You wish to pile on to that?" I ask.

"I don't think anyone is trying to pile on. I was just going to say if she's worth it, put the work in. Trust me. Walking away because of ego, pride, or past will never be the answer. All it gets you is a half-full life." With that, Aiden stands, throws down some money, and juts his chin out toward Chase in a silent thank you.

"Okay, fess up," I say to Chase once Aiden leaves. "Who is that guy? Because I *know* I've seen him before, and it's driving me crazy."

Chase looks around before leaning in. "He's a friend of my brother, James." He shifts back up, shrugging.

There has to be more to Aiden than merely being a friend of Chase's brother. I stare at Chase for a moment, and it clicks. "Holy hell, that's Aiden Cox, catcher for the Philadelphia Legends."

"Shh, keep it down. I am aware of who he is."

"What the hell is Aiden Cox hanging out in your bar for?"

"Thanks, ass. What's wrong with my bar?" He glares at me. "James told him to escape everything going on back in Philadelphia. So, he's staying in James's apartment in Portland while things get worked out with his team. The guy just needs a place to go, and I promised him he'd have one here. That's all."

"I still can't believe your brother is some hotshot professional baseball player."

"Yeah, well, I can. He never lets me forget it." Chase fills a pint. "Back on topic, are you going to go get the girl?"

"Nah, man, not now."

"Seriously? Don't be stupid," he scolds.

I want to argue with him. But as I open my mouth, I notice his gaze continuously going toward the opposite end of the bar. I follow it to find Gretchen.

After blowing out a deep breath, I stand and put my coat back on. I pull out enough to cover my drinks and at least a round for Gretchen. "This is for mine, and whatever Gretchen orders. And I'm not being stupid. I'm realizing that before I try to get around her walls and issues, I have to deal with my own."

29

JULES

"Gretchen? Are you home?" I call.

"In my room."

After putting my bags down in our front room, I go to her bedroom, searching for some comfort.

"Hey, hon. You look awful," she says.

It's true. My eyes are swollen and red from all the crying I've been doing. Still, I pick up one of her decorative pillows and toss it at her. It totally misses her. I can't get anything correct right now. "I lost him. Actually, I can't even say that. Because he left. I told him to go, and he didn't even put up a fight. I told him he won't find anyone better."

I hiccup. Apparently, I'm not out of tears, because more fall down my face.

"Damn right he won't." She gets up off the floor where it looks like she was going through mementos and opens her arms to me.

I fling back on her bed instead, choosing to hug one of her pillows.

"Want to tell me what happened?" she asks.

I blow out a breath and look at her, silently thanking God

that I have her in my life. She has been there for me, as much as I've let anyone be. I open my mouth to try to explain my weekend, but a sound like a cat being eaten by a coyote is all that comes out.

"You know you're correct, right?" she says. "He won't find someone better than you. Did he say that to you? That he wanted something or someone better? I will kill him. I'm serious. I might hang with six and seven-year-olds the majority of my day, but that doesn't mean I won't kill someone."

"No, he didn't say anything like that. I mean, I told him he wouldn't ever have better. But what…what if I won't either?" Tears pour down my face, soaking the neck of my shirt. I'm a hot mess right now.

I hiccup again before continuing. "I know I deserve better. But I love him, and I pretty much told him that. If I'm being honest, if he walked in that door right now," I say, pointing to Gretchen's bedroom door, "I'd be pissed. So pissed. But if he apologized, I'd take it and I'd love him and never look back. How pathetic am I?"

"Hey. Shut up. You're talking about my best friend. That is not pathetic, it's honest. And I'm not sticking up for him, but from what Chase said, Hunter hasn't been acting the same. So, even if he didn't say it, I'd bet my life he loves you too."

I carefully play with the beads on my bracelet. The thread broke yesterday, and I had to tie a knot in the string to keep it together. "You and Chase talked about us?"

"Your vague texts over the weekend had me wondering, so I went to Portland Social to see Chase and find out if he knew anything. It surprised me to see Hunter at the end of the bar. I could tell something was off. I started walking over to him, but Chase saw me and shook his head for me not to. So, I didn't. Hunter left shortly after that. But Chase told me Hunter was in an awful place, mentally."

This makes my heart ache. I'm jealous Gretchen got to see

198 | QUINN MILLER

Hunter. I want to see him so badly. To hear that he's hurting tears me up inside. *Is he hurting as much as I am? If so, why is he doing this to us?*

I take a deep breath and wipe my face. Then I lift my eyes and look at Gretchen. "As much as I want to bring him back to me, the fact remains that he walked away. It doesn't matter his reasons or how much of what he said was or wasn't true. He left me there. I was begging him, and he walked away. I told him he made me fall in love with him. He was so wonderful I felt like I had no choice but to fall. I admit I have my hang-ups and walls, but that bastard got around it all."

"What are you going to do?" She bites on the side of her nail, almost as if my answer will have some outcome in *her* life.

"I'm going to give myself some grace. I'm going to live in this heartbreak tonight. Tomorrow, I'll get up, exercise, and go to work. I will keep on doing that until I don't have to force myself. I will keep on living. And I will hope that one day, hopefully not too far away, I will love him less. Maybe at some point I will meet someone new, and *they* will be my future. Even though that person won't be who I want *now*, I hope I will honestly be able to look at that man—and without thinking of Hunter—tell my *future* person that I love him completely."

Gretchen looks at me, mouth agape. "Damn, girl. Can I be you when I grow up? Because, personally, I'd be living at the bottom of a Ben and Jerry's container for a while, listening to love songs and yelling at sappy movies."

Laughing, I grab her and hold her. "Well, Ben and Jerry's sounds pretty good right now." But then, my mind goes to when I very recently went searching for solace at the bottom of a pint.

"Oh, Jules, where did you just go?" Gretchen asks. "Your entire body is trembling."

Remembering my talk with my mom about how I need to let more people in, I take a deep breath and turn to my friend. "There's someone I want to tell you about."

I then share with Gretchen the story of me and Matt. Finally.

# 30

## HUNTER

### TWO MONTHS LATER...

*T*he people on the streets as I walk into Portland Social appear happy. There's something about Oregonians. They seem to appreciate beautiful, sunny days more than others. This spring day just feels like a good day.

It's still early, but the bar has a crowd for Friday afternoon. I take the sole stool left at the bar. Holly—the pretty, redheaded bartender that works here—comes over to see what I'd like. As she makes my drink, our friendly banter comes easy.

"Stop hitting on my employee, Hunter," booms Chase.

I shake my head as he comes around the bar, asking her to go check on some tables. "Why? Are you sleeping with her?"

"Nope. She's too valuable here to mess it up with a fun night or two."

"Oh, funny boys. Flirting is harmless. Trust me, I like my men interested in only me, not hung up on other girls," Holly singsongs as she passes me my drink.

"Ah, fuck me," Chase mutters.

I laugh. "Chill, Chase. I think she's just messing with us."

Chase grabs the back of his neck as he keeps looking

between me and then over my head. "I wasn't talking about Holly. Just promise me you're going to be calm, okay?"

"What the hell are you talking about?"

"Look over your shoulder at the group that just sat at one of the high bar tables. Last stool on the right, her back is to us."

I set my drink down and turn my head to look. There she is.

I haven't seen Jules since the trip to her parents' house. She's as breathtakingly beautiful as ever, though she never notices the effect she has on men. Just by a quick glance, I can see five other guys in this place checking her out. I have no right to be jealous, but it makes me feel that way. She's *mine*. But she isn't. Not anymore. I made sure I eviscerated that bridge.

She hasn't seen me yet, so I take my fill of her. I can't help the smile that takes over my face when I hear her laughter. One of the guys she's with leans in, places his hand on her lower back, and pulls her a bit toward him. He whispers something in her ear, and she laughs again. *Fucker.* I don't know who he is, but I can't stand him.

Her hair is in loose waves. Her black skirt she has on, I bet it hugs her ass perfectly. Unfortunately, she's sitting on the stool so I can't enjoy it. She uncrosses her left ankle from over her right, then crosses her right over her left, her legs dangling. She's wearing heels today. She keeps talking with the guy next to her and touching his bicep.

I was in such a good mood when I walked in here. Now, I want to hit someone. I turn back around to Chase, and he jumps back.

"Whoa, killer. No punishing the bar owner and deliverer of news. I am sorry, though. When was the last time you saw her?" he asks.

"That weekend at her parents' place. Shit. I thought I was doing okay. But honestly, Chase, when I wake up each day it's like I can still feel her body next to mine. And seeing her..." I shake my head and run my fingers through my hair. "Seeing her is messing with me more than I thought it would." I look over my shoulder again. "She looks incredible. Who's the guy with her?"

"Man, I have no clue. Really, though, what did you think it would be like if you saw her again? You're clearly in love with her."

*What did I think?* I didn't *want* to think about it. I didn't want to picture her because, like a true masochist, whenever I think of her, I picture her blushing and breathless underneath me. Her nails digging into me as I thrust. Her gaze fixated on me as my name escapes her gorgeous mouth like a prayer. But I can't say any of that or I'll look crazy.

So I tell him, "I didn't think I'd run into her. I felt the odds were on my side."

Chase tosses down a bar towel. "Stay here. I'll be right back."

It takes every ounce of strength to keep my gaze forward. But I do. It seems like hours before Chase returns.

"What did you do?" I ask him.

"Nothing. I helped Holly take their drinks over. It would have been rude of me not to say hi."

"And?"

"And they all work together, I think. She seems good."

I toss back my drink and ask Chase to make me another. While he gets it, I place my hands on the ice on the bar to try to cool off. It isn't working. I hear her laugh again, and my gut knots. I toss back my next drink once he hands it to me and then I stand.

"Hey, man. Please don't cause any trouble, okay?" Chase begs. "Don't do or say something you're going to regret."

"Oh, ye of little faith. Trust." I turn and walk over to her group.

I put both hands in my pockets so I won't do anything stupid like touch her, and I stand beside her. "Hey, Jules," I say, drawing her attention. "It's nice to see you."

*Nice to see you?* Ugh, that was lame.

She turns and acts shocked to see me, but her eyes betray her. She knew I was here. *Interesting.* "Hunter, hi. How are you?"

I try to focus on her, but I see the guy on the other side of her run his hand up and down her arm. My hands form into fists in my pockets. *Why the hell did I come over here?* "I'm well. You?"

"I'm good. Just celebrating the end of the week."

I nod and look at the other people with her before looking at her again. "Where's Gretchen?"

Her eyes dip, and she looks sad.

I want nothing more than to comfort her. Before I can think twice about it, I take my hand out of my pocket.

I raise her chin with my finger and thumb so she looks at me. "Everything okay?"

"There was an emergency with her grandma, so she left work early."

"I'm sorry to hear that. Please let me know if they need anything."

She closes her eyes briefly before looking up at me again. "Thank you, Hunter." She reaches for her water and takes a sip. I tilt my head slightly.

She leans closer to me. "I'm trying to be more authentic." She sits up straighter on her stool. There's no back to lean against.

It's obvious no one she's with would understand what we're talking about. But it isn't lost on me. I've missed the way she's looking at me now. It's a mixture of interest and hope.

Hell, I miss her with all that I am. *How did I epically screw this up?* I don't know what else to say to her now. I messed up my chance with her. "Well, enjoy your time. It was nice seeing you, Jules." Before she can say anything, I walk back to the bar.

Chase walks over to me. "So?"

"Not now, okay. I just wanted to give you a heads up to give Gretchen a call. You say nothing is going on with you two, but whether you admit it or not, you care about her. And from what Jules just said, Gretchen might need a friend. Something about her grandmother."

"Shit. Her grandma raised her. Thanks for telling me."

"Sure." I stand and pay him for my drinks and tell him I'll catch him later.

I keep my head down as I walk past Jules. Seeing her is harder than I expected. Walking back outside, the sunny day doesn't seem as jovial and promising as it did when I had first walked in. Today went from pleasant to painful, quickly.

I want her to be happy. I'm just selfish and want her happy with *me*.

She has my heart. I was an idiot for pushing her away.

31

HUNTER

"*H*unter." I hear my name being yelled.

For a moment, I think I'm imagining it.

"Hunter!" she yells again.

I stop and turn to see Jules running toward me. I don't move. I should walk to her, but I am cemented where I am.

She stops in front of me, putting a finger up for me to wait as she calms her breathing. "Sorry." Breath. "I wasn't planning on running in..." She kicks up her foot and points to her heel. She stands before me, smiling.

My heart hammers against my chest. Waiting.

"Will, the guy sitting next to me, I'm not seeing him. I just —" She messes with her hair and looks down the street before looking at me again. "He was trying to make you jealous. I didn't ask him to," she rushes. "I saw you the second I walked into the bar and Will was just, being Will. It was stupid and childish. I'm sorry. I didn't want you to think I was interested in him. God, I'm just rambling. I'm going to shut up." She bites her upper lip while looking up at me, pleading.

I hesitate for a second before deciding to be honest. "It worked."

Jules quirks an eyebrow. "What worked?"

"Will. He made me jealous. Crazy jealous."

She smiles, and I want to kiss her. But I have no right to.

"This may be stupid of me, but hell, I don't want to walk away from you again with regrets," I say. "I have so many regrets from the weekend at your parents'. I overreacted. But I didn't know how to come to you after everything I said. I am so damn sorry."

"I think we both made some mistakes." She steps closer to me and takes hold of both my hands.

"Jules, you have my heart. If there's even the smallest chance you want me, please tell me now, because I will do everything in my power to love you the way you deserve."

"Do you think you could stop talking and kiss me?" she says.

"What? Why? Actually, ignore all that—I don't know why I'm even questioning you."

She puts her hand over my mouth. "Hunter, stop talking and just kiss me."

My hands move to her lower back, pulling her to me, erasing any space that's left between us.

She looks up at me, grinning, and I just look into her beautiful ocean eyes for a minute. I've missed getting lost in their depths. And then, all restraint snaps, and I crash my mouth into hers. She opens her mouth for me, and our tongues dance.

I pull back. "Humor me, okay? I want us to do this right. So go home and be ready in two hours. I'll have my driver pick you up."

"What are you planning?" She looks at me cautiously.

"Just be prepared. I want to show you how much you mean to me. I'll see you soon." I let go of her hands and take a step back.

"You know, it would be easier if you come back home with me and show me now," she flirts.

"Nah, when you find your *forever*, you don't go for easy. I'll see you soon, beautiful. I promise." I have the biggest grin on my face.

Sunny spring days truly are the best. At least, when you have the one you love.

AFTER SAYING goodbye to Jules on the sidewalk, I call my driver Frank to come pick me up. I have two hours to plan an evening worthy of Jules. She isn't someone who asks for a lot, but she is definitely someone who deserves it. Her coming after me today might be the bravest thing I've ever seen her do. I know how hard it is for her to be vulnerable.

It gives me the courage I need. I've been so scared of staying in one place and letting people truly see me. I now own and run Steeple Investments. There's no reason for me to still be running all around, traveling as much as I do. But I always felt like I had to prove myself to others.

It's time I stop running and actually prove myself where it matters.

With Jules, I need to trust in us. Chase was right. I am not my parents. I need to stop making myself pay for their mistakes.

"You look happy, sir," Frank comments as we work our way through downtown traffic.

"I am." I look out the window as we stop at a light and see something in a window that I know will look amazing on Jules. I have Frank pull over, and I sprint into the boutique.

By the time we leave the store and make it back to my house, I have an hour until Jules will arrive. In an hour, my future starts.

# JULES

*a* s I make it into my apartment, I remove my shoes and toss my keys into the dish. *What just happened?* A part of me can't believe I chased after him. He left Portland Social looking so sad. I had promised myself if he looked at me as he walked out the door, I'd tell him how much I've missed him. He never looked, but somehow that only spurred me more. So, I gave the quickest goodbye to my coworkers and ran. I heard someone yell, "It's about damn time," as I opened the door. Chase. *Adorable asshole.*

But now, I'm here by myself. *What the actual—*

My phone pings with a text, and my doorbell rings. I choose the door over my phone, hoping I'll find Hunter on the other side.

I don't. Instead, I see a man with an ostentatious display of floral magic. My face hurts from my smile.

"Ms. Morgan?"

"Yes."

"These are for you, miss. From Mr. Peterson."

If possible, my smile spreads further. I wrap my hands around the enormous arrangement of honeysuckles and tulips.

"Thank you." I push my front door closed and walk toward the kitchen.

"Miss," the deliveryman says, putting his foot out to stop the door from closing. "There is more."

"What?" *Oh Lord. Hunter what did you do?* "Just a minute, let me put these down. I'm so sorry." I rush into the kitchen and place the flower arrangement on our island and quickly return to the deliveryman.

"Here you go, miss." He hands me two shopping bags.

I turn to grab money for a tip out of my purse, but he assures me it's been taken care of.

So I say goodbye and hurry to my room with my packages. It feels like Christmas morning. I pull out the tissue-wrapped items, and a card falls out of the second bag.

*MY JULES,*

*I'm sorry I'm not better planned for this. I've been an idiot the last few weeks. You can wear what you want, but I saw this and thought of you. I apologize if they don't fit. I hope you like it all. Now hurry and get ready. Frank will bring you to my house. I can't wait to have you in my arms again.*

*With everything,*
*Hunter*

NOPE, this is better than Christmas morning. I grab my cell before getting ready.

**Me:** You are crazy. *And* amazing.

**Hunter:** Are you happy?

**Me:** Unbelievably so. See you soon.

*Soon* turns into just over an hour. It takes a bit of prep to look exceptional enough for the dress he picked out—and the undergarments he bought.

I've never had a guy buy me underwear before. I have to say, it's one hell of a turn-on. After I am officially buffed, shaved, lotioned, and styled, I meet Frank down at the curb.

I THINK it's time for me to take control of what I can control and let the rest just happen. My future is on the other side of this door. All six-foot-four of him. Before I can knock, the door opens. And standing there in a tailored navy suit, is Hunter.

"I was too impatient to wait for you to knock. Goddamn, you are gorgeous," he says.

Feeling brave, I teasingly say, "If you like this, you should see how what you picked out for underneath looks." And then I smile.

Hunter is still standing too far from me for my liking. "I told myself we'd talk first, but hell, I can't wait any longer." He makes it to me in one long stride. The kiss is languid and sensual.

With my heels, our height difference isn't as great.

I break our kiss and pull him down so I can whisper in his ear. "The best thing you can do for us right now is to connect us. Because Hunter, I love you, and I want you. Only you." I pull back and he gives me the best smile I have ever seen.

"Say it again," he all but growls.

I look into his eyes and with a full hear, I say, "I love you."

His mouth is on mine, kissing over my jaw, down my neck. He grabs both sides of my face and then he pulls back slightly, looking right at me. "I love you too, Jules."

I close my eyes and give myself a moment to bask in those words. "Show me," I breathe out.

Two simple words from me, and we both know any conversation we need to have can wait.

# HUNTER

*S*o, on that glorious spring day, I made love to the love of my life, and damn, was it the best day of my life thus far.

When morning comes, Jules asks, "Where do we start?"

I divulge the truth about my parents and their accident. I share my misplaced fears about her learning of my own hidden past. I tell her about growing up with Benjamin and how I came to live with him. She's understanding and caring, with all of it.

Lastly, I share with Jules that she's the first person to say she loves me.

We both regret how her declaration had gone down. I apologize to her for not trusting fully in us.

But we can't change our past. We can learn from it and move on, striving to be better. I love this woman, and I'm going to make sure I not only tell her, but also show her as often as I can.

Then it's her turn. I squeeze her hand, letting her know I'm here for her, and she begins.

"I went from feeling like my life was limitless to having nothing," she says. "I realize I didn't have *nothing*, but that's how it felt. So, I tried to control everything I could. I didn't comprehend how it dictated my life." She lets go of my hand and points to me with a genuine smile on her face. "You were so not in my plan, Hunter."

"Do you think you can add me in, say, for life?" I touch the back of her neck to bring her toward me, pulling her onto my lap so she's straddling me. "Calm down, love. I'm not going to ask you to marry me—yet."

I give her a quick kiss. "*But,* one day, I am going to ask you to be my wife. I want this, Jules. I want you. I want our future. I want you to be mine and me yours. I want to raise kids with you. Do you think you can handle all of that?"

She looks around the room like she's seeing if she can picture herself here, in my life. "I thought for so long that Matt was the love of my life. We barely had a relationship, but it still shaped so much of who I am. My tattoo—"

"On your ribs? The butterflies?"

"Yes. I got them when I moved here. Matt called me his butterfly. It was just once, on the day he died. He never explained it. When I moved to Portland, it was the first time I felt like I was moving forward. I didn't want to forget my past, though. So I put a piece of it on my body. Because it all makes up who I am."

My hand goes to where her tattoo is, and my fingers trace over the area. "You've been like a butterfly, always outside my grasp. But I promise to be still, and be a place for you to rest."

"Matt was my first love. But, Hunter, you're the love of my life. I want everything with you that you promised. I want our future."

I cup her face in my hands. "You are my everything."

"I want to show you something." She bites her upper lip as she moves to retrieve something. Then, she hands over a book.

I look down at the album and then at Jules with raised eyebrows. "What is it, love?"

"It's the last Christmas present I received from my brother.

My parents always encouraged us to make our gifts for each other. When we were little, I remember one year asking him what his favorite animal was, and for Christmas that year, I drew him a picture of it. I'm sure it looked awful, but my mom always said it's the thought that counts." She shrugs and looks nervously between me and the album now in my hands.

I put an arm around her, bringing her in closer to me, then I kiss her forehead.

"I thought you could look at this and get a little glimpse into who Mitch was, and what our relationship looked like. He was the best brother."

"I love that you brought this. Thank you for trusting me with it," I say.

Her eyes glisten as she looks at me. "I knew you'd understand what it meant to me—showing this to you, I mean. I wish Mitch could have met you, but just maybe, he's looking down with Matt and they both see how happy I am. And, how special you are."

I pause flipping through the pages to look at her. "I hope they are." I know how huge this is, her sharing this with me, and it means more to me than I can express.

Calm settles over us and she fills me in on family jokes and stories. We spend the rest of the afternoon trading stories about our pasts.

After we close the book, I reach over her and put it in the nightstand drawer on her side of the bed.

"Don't worry, I won't keep it. But it's safe there until you take it home. Consider that your drawer now." I kiss the tip of her nose.

She nods her head then leans toward me and starts to kiss my neck. "I think we made big strides today with sharing our histories, but I'm all talked out. Make love to me, Hunter, please."

We spend the rest of the day making love and making up for the time we missed being together.

By the time we wake the next day, it is late morning. I pull her into me.

"Do you want to see if Gretchen is back and wants to meet us at Portland Social?" I ask.

"I've been texting with her," Jules says. "She's still at her grandma's and probably will be for a few days, but I'd still love to go. We can order some yummy spinach artichoke dip and chat with Chase before he gets too busy."

"Play darts?" I hint.

She looks at me with one raised eyebrow and a hand on her hip as she stands up from the bed. She's still naked, so the pissed-off stance doesn't absolutely hit where she wants it to. But *damn,* she looks marvelous.

"I am not playing darts with you again. You play dirty. I saw he put in a shuffleboard table, though. We could play that if it's available."

"Sounds good, love. Let's get ready. First, how about we shower?"

"Oh no, you have *that* look. You are insatiable." She takes off for the bathroom, filling the room with her laughter.

WHEN WE FINALLY MAKE IT to Portland Social, we see Holly at the bar.

"Hey, Holly. Chase in the back? Or is he actually taking a day off?"

"No, sorry. He said something about a family emergency."

"He left you alone at the bar with no help?"

"Nah, he's been training a guy, so we just kind of skipped the rest of training and went to the sink-or-swim method. Things have been okay."

Jules and I order drinks and the appetizer she wanted. Holly fills our drink order and lets us know she will bring over the appetizer when it's ready. We take our drinks over to the unoccupied shuffleboard table. As competitive as we are, this will be interesting.

"Chase isn't here? I hope everything is okay," Jules says.

"Yeah, it's weird he didn't text me about it. I'll send him one and see what's up."

As I text him, Jules salts the table and gets ready.

"Huh...well, I'll be damned," I mumble.

She walks up next to me and peers around my arm. "What's up?"

I turn my phone to show her.

**Me:** At PS and you aren't. Holly mentioned a family emergency. Is everything okay?

**Chase:** Yeah, I'm with Gretchen.

Jules and I look at each other, both wearing a smirk. We talked about them over the weekend, comparing notes and trying to figure out what—if anything—is going on with them.

"I told you something was up with those two." She moves around the table and resets the score so we can start.

"I never disagreed. But doesn't look like we'll get any answers today."

Holly comes over and drops off our appetizer.

"So, shall we make a bet?" I wiggle my eyebrows.

Jules laughs while shaking her head. "Oh, no. You and your bets."

"Hey, that last bet worked out well for both of us." Laughter flows easily from me. I have a feeling life will hold a lot more laughter and joy going forward. I pull Jules toward me. "Afraid?"

"Nah, whatever you come up with, either way it falls, we'll both enjoy it." She gazes at me with those beautiful blues.

"After already having my way with you, you still think I need to win a bet to get you to sleep with me?"

"Oh, please. We've had our way with each other. And I don't think you need to win a bet to, but I'm pretty sure whatever bet you throw down will involve nakedness later."

"Well, you are wrong."

"Oh Lord." She rolls her eyes at me. "Let me hear it."

"Loser has to propose to the winner within the next six months." It's bold, and I don't want to scare her, but I know what I want. It simply boils down to a *forever* with her.

She doesn't hesitate, though. With the biggest smile, she says, "You're on."

# EPILOGUE

Jules
*Almost Six Months Later...*

The bar's so packed, I wonder if the fire department will pay Chase a visit.

"Stop stressing." Gretchen sidles up next to me. "And stop playing with your bracelet. There's nothing to worry about. Tonight will be perfect." She covers my hand to force me to stop. "At least Hunter gave you an upgrade."

I look down at the beautiful Claddagh and Celtic knot bracelet Hunter picked out for me on our travels. We were in Ireland when my beaded bracelet finally broke beyond repair.

Over the summer, while I was off, I accompanied Hunter on a month-long vacation. The first one he ever took that didn't involve work.

The first two weeks were spent traveling around France and London. The final two weeks we spent in Ireland. At a little

218 | QUINN MILLER

shop, he found my new bracelet. I had mentioned how much I liked Gretchen's ring with the Claddagh symbol.

"I am not stressing," I say, and Gretchen gives me a pointed look. "I'm not! But I am nervous. This is a big night. I want it to go well."

"You and Hunter have been working on this for months. It will be great. Now relax."

Just then, I spot Hunter. He's better than any drink could ever be at calming my nerves.

"Oh, hell, lady. Wait until the end of the night when you two are safely behind doors at home!"

Yep, before our trip, I moved into Hunter's house. He told me he didn't want to come home anymore and not have me with him. I was sad to no longer live with Gretchen, but I knew we'd still see each other at work.

Chase, Gretchen, Hunter, and I started having Sunday brunch at Portland Social every week. Chase was expanding his menu offerings, and it was the perfect meeting spot for all of us.

Gretchen groans now as Hunter weaves his way through the crowd, coming closer to us.

"What? I did nothing," I say as innocently as possible.

"Please, I could smell the sex pheromones wafting off you the instant you spotted him. You get this goofy look. Your face is all stupid happy."

"Jealous, Gretch? And what exactly is *stupid happy*?" But I can feel the goofy smile on my face. I can't help it. I am so ecstatic in our relationship.

"Hell yes, I'm jealous. You get mind-blowing sex on the regular. No wonder you have that perma-grin around him. But more so, I'm elated for you. You deserve it. Plus, I get weekly coffee out of it, so I'm good." She gives me a one-arm hug.

Yep, Hunter has kept up with his weekly Friday coffee delivery at my school. This school year, he added in a muffin for me. Gretchen now gets her own coffee and breakfast too. What can I say? He's a smart man and knows to get on well with the best friend.

I see Hunter walking toward us, and my smile overtakes my face.

"Hello, ladies. Is this where the beautiful people are hanging out?"

"It was until you showed up," Chase jokes as he comes up behind us. He puts his arm around me before Hunter can claim me, and I rest my head against his right shoulder and laugh at his antics.

Hunter peers at us, practically growling.

Chase finally relinquishes his hold on me, and I walk into Hunter's waiting arms.

"Are you ready to get the show on the road, love?" Hunter squeezes the back of my neck.

"I am if you are." With that, we link hands and walk over to the stage.

Chase listened to me and Gretch when we suggested doing some open mic nights here to draw a crowd. But tonight, Hunter said the performers are a surprise.

Hunter walks to the mic and says, "Hello, everyone. If I may grab your attention for a moment."

I watch as all the patrons turn toward his commanding voice. So many familiar faces. My parents are beaming while watching Hunter. Next to them are Matt's parents. Paula and I have kept in touch. It's been a healthy healing for both of us. I've had limited contact with Eric, and the few times were strained. He came tonight. I have yet to talk to him, though.

"First, I want to thank everyone for joining us to support this cause. When Jules and I had the idea for the Mitch Matthew scholarship, it was just that—an idea. But together, we can all make it a reality."

I beam at him. It already is a reality.

Not only is he good with a crowd, but he's being kind, stating this was *our* idea. It was all him. He came to me once he'd already set it all up and had donated $100,000 of his own money. Tonight, though, he's invited a lot of clients and business associates so the scholarship can grow. It's for high school seniors, and it's not limited to college.

We worked on the wording together. We know college isn't everyone's dream, so we made sure it'd be available to kids who want to go to trade school, police or fire academy, or really *anything* post high school. The opportunities are limitless.

I walk over to my parents as Hunter continues with his speech.

"Honey, this is astounding. Thank you again for honoring your brother like this." My mom gets teary-eyed and chokes up.

"Thank you for being here tonight. It means so much to us." I hug my mom and glance over at my dad, who gives me a wink.

"Your mother and I are so proud of you, Jules. The best thing for any parent is to see their child happy. Not only are you happy but you are channeling that joy into helping others." My dad starts to get emotional. Instead of letting him say anything more, I give him a hug.

"Without further delay, I want to introduce the amazing, talented recording artist: We Three."

My mouth hangs open. Hunter told me he booked a group for tonight but refused to tell me which one. I tried my confession methods on him, but he wouldn't break. Hunter knows I love the Oregon band—even since *before* they were on America's Got Talent.

The two brothers and their sister grace the small stage. They greet their audience and start their set with my current favorite song, *Hold Me, Baby*.

Hunter comes up behind me and sways with me in his arms. I turn to him and wrap my arms around his neck, pulling him in for a kiss. It isn't nearly the kiss he deserves, but my parents are right behind me. We dance to the band singing about love and butterflies.

Hunter twirls me, yet when I come back around to him, I have to stare down, as he kneels before me. *Oh Jesus.*

His handsome face smiles up at me with so much joy. "Love, you are my future. The best thing I ever did was come into this very bar almost a year ago. Promise me your future and say yes. Be my wife. Be in my life as my partner, forever."

I don't even try to hide the tears as I gaze into his hazel eyes. I notice they are even getting teary. I put a hand on each side of his face and lean down so close he can probably feel my breath against his lips. "You already have me, but my answer is yes. Always yes. I love you so much, Hunter. I can't wait to become Jules Peterson."

"I love how that sounds." With both of us crying and smiling, Hunter slips on the emerald-cut sapphire ring flanked with a diamond on each side and accent diamonds down the platinum band.

My breath stutters when I admire the most gorgeous ring I have ever seen.

"If you don't like it, it's your mom's fault," he jokes.

I look behind me at my mom, shocked. She's usually a horrid secret keeper, but somehow, she kept one this huge. "*You knew?*"

She eyes me coyly and smiles. "Hunter called and asked if I'd like to go with him. Really, I did nothing other than cry the whole afternoon. He picked it out. He almost passed out when he saw it." She grabs my hand and holds up my finger with my new accessory. "He knew right away when he saw it."

I hug both my parents. Then I turn and scream like an idiot and wave my hand around to show Gretchen. We embrace and jump around in a circle like schoolgirls.

When I feel a tap on my shoulder, I turn to see Eric. My smile fades a bit as I brace myself.

"Congratulations, Jules. Genuinely. It's nice to see you so happy." His gaze goes momentarily to Hunter, giving him a nod before he turns his attention back to me. "Your happiness is all I ever wanted."

Eric turns to leave, but I stop him. "Thank you, Eric. That means a lot to me. I hope you find happiness too."

He gives me a smile and turns to walk over to his parents.

Hunter wraps me in his arms and whispers in my ear, "Are you happy, love?"

Gazing into his hazel eyes, I see my future. "So unbelievably happy. Thank you, Hunter, for loving me the way you do. I can't wait to continue building our lives together."

He leans down and kisses me. As usual with us, we get a bit caught up in the moment.

"Dude, hold that till later. There are parents in the room." Chase slaps a hand on each of our backs, breaking our kiss. "Cutting it a bit close, aren't you?"

I roll my eyes. He's referring to my bet with Hunter back in April.

As usual, I beat Hunter that day, giving *him* six months to propose. I have to admit, I didn't think he'd wait as long as he did.

"Stop worrying about my love life, dude, and focus on your own," Hunter teases.

I can see Chase as he glances over to Gretchen. She avoids him and peers down at her shoes. I hope they can work their story out.

Hunter is oblivious to it all as he only has eyes for me. "This had nothing to do with a bet. I wanted tonight to be about you. I wanted you to know your past is still a part of us and always will be. I love you, Jules, and I will never stop showing you."

I'm walking out of here tonight with my fiancé. We both had a bumpy road to reach each other, but everything that has happened has brought us here. God, so much can change in under an hour, in the best of ways.

# ACKNOWLEDGMENTS

*"Romance? Really?"*

It's a common reaction I got when I announced I was writing my first book.

My love for the genre started a few years ago. However, the books I've been drawn to and the writing I've done in the past always had romantic elements that I loved.

A few years ago, I went down the rabbit hole. I was home sick with an awful flu and found a book by Cristin Harber—part of her Titan Series. I devoured the entire series and all of her other books. I then stumbled upon Erin Nicholas, then Adriana Locke, to Teagan Hunter, Kate Stewart, Ilsa Madden-Mills, and so on. These six will always hold a special place in my heart, though.

So, *"Romance? Really?"* Yes. It's an escape for me. A world I can visit when reality gets a little too real. But in a way, as cheesy as I know this sounds, I get to fall in love with my husband repeatedly. He's the love of my life. So, thank you to other writers, but especially these six, for giving me an escape with your amazing words and inspiring me. I encourage you, if you haven't already, to check them out.

This book wouldn't be in your hands if not for the following people:

Alessandra Torre. Without you and Inkers, I don't know if I would have had the guts to do this. Thank you, in a year as memorable as 2020, for still pulling off the new writers' bootcamp.

Sandra, thank you for helping shape my words.

Christina, thank you for making me laugh with your commentary while simultaneously making me want to cry over all the edits.

Amanda, Jen, and Tori, for a last look and making the pages look pretty.

Shannon, for making the cover I had hoped for come true.

Ena at Enticing Journey, for helping get this book seen.

To my amazing beta readers—Nicki Holt, Laura Jackson, Stephanie Obrey, Becky, Linda, and Terryl—for being the first eyes to see this book.

Thank you to my sister, who has been an amazing support and incredible example for me. I love you, Heather.

Thank you to you, my readers. I am humbled that, out of all the options, you clicked on my book. Thank you!

Last, but never least, to my husband. Thank you for encouraging me to do this. Thank you for listening to my ramblings and giving me the time to dedicate to my craft. I love you madly.

# ABOUT THE AUTHOR

*Better Days* is Quinn Miller's debut novel. She lives in the Pacific Northwest with her two daughters, husband, and dog, who her husband refers to as her boyfriend.

Instagram: Author Quinn Miller
Facebook: Author Quinn Miller
Facebook Reader Group: Miller Social
Twitter: Author Quinn Miller
Email: authorquinnmiller@gmail.com
Spotify Playlist: Better Days

Want to find out what happens between Gretchen and Chase? Click here to sign up for my newsletter!

Made in the USA
Monee, IL
24 March 2021

63698384R00135